ZERO JUDGMENT

Tales from the Tarot

Kota Quinn

Zero Judgment
Copyright © 2024 – Kota Quinn

All rights reserved.

No part of this publication may be reproduced, distributed, or transmitted in any form or by any means, including photocopying, recording, or other electronic or mechanical methods, without the prior written permission of the publisher, except in the case of brief quotations embodied in critical reviews and certain other noncommercial uses permitted by copyright law.

Cover art: Fae Quin
Cover design: Amanda Meuwissen
Book layout: Amanda Meuwissen
Beta Reader: Morgan Lysand
Editing by: JennReadsMMBooks.com

Printed in the United States of America

JUDGMENT

XX

JUDGMENT

BLURB

Zero is a tracker for the Elite Guard, the supernatural police that hunts down rogues. Zero's number one goal was to work for the Elite and seek revenge on the vampires who killed his childhood friend.

But after so many years of moving from place to place, he wants to settle down. Zero volunteers to help guard one of the magical small towns where paranormals and humans live together openly.

He's settled in this new town, has a life, friends, and hopefully, soon he'll meet his mate. But what he doesn't expect to find is his childhood friend alive and well. Except his friend isn't alive. He's undead, just like all the creatures he's hunted down.

Zero Judgment is a standalone MM romance novel as part of the multi-author collaboration Tales from the Tarot. This book is based on the major arcana card Judgment.

To my husband
Your support this year has meant the world to me.

and

To Nikki
We love you and miss you every day.

AUTHOR'S NOTE

Let me begin by expressing my sincere thanks to my family and my husband. Writing this book has been a difficult journey with its fair share of challenges. While Zero's story was something I've seen clearly for over a year, my personal life decided to prevent me from being near my laptop. Even though there are so many other scenes of Calix and Zero living in my head, I'm very proud of the story I was able to produce during this difficult time. I fully expect Zero and Calix to make cameos in future stories, and who knows, maybe I can expand their romance.

Another reason this story means so much to me is because the meaning of the Judgment card is interwoven throughout this whole story. Now, while some might think that the card is just about not judging others or even themselves, it's so much more. It's about feeling that inner calling, that intuition that guides you somewhere. It's also about rebirth and starting a new chapter in our lives.

Don't be afraid to chase after your dream and follow your soul's true calling.

TRIGGER WARNINGS

Implied SA and Dubcon
MC kidnapped

Spoiler Alert: Calix was kidnapped at the age of fifteen by vampires who planned on using him as a human blood bag. (Off page.)

Murdering evil vampires who deserve so much worse.

Nothing happens to him sexually until he is nineteen. (Off page.) The story opens up when that same character is thirty.

Chapter One
CALIX

Like the obedient husband I'm supposed to be, I wait for Helios to return home from his feeding. He'll be back any moment now, after tormenting whoever he pleases—likely wreaking havoc on some poor human before draining them dry.

It's expected for us, as creatures of the night, to possess control and grace. Only the weak are unable to control their blood lust. According to vampire beliefs, our ability to control our urges should strengthen with age. Well, Helios is old as fuck, and yet he only gets worse the older he gets. That lack of control disgusts me.

He disgusts me.

As if summoned by the gates of hell, the door opens and Helios strides in. "Calix, my love. You look gorgeous tonight." He clicks the door closed behind him and shrugs out of his bloody jacket. "Already on the bed, eagerly awaiting me, I see."

My cheeks flame, and I bite back my smart-ass remark. I'm on the bed because he demands it, nothing more. When my eyes trail up his pants and see he isn't tenting his trousers, I relax, letting him see a smile on my face. He must have gotten his rocks off with the human. I just pray he didn't kill the innocent thing.

"How was your feeding tonight, husband?" I ask, trying to ignore my own hunger. *Being a little hungry every once in a while is good for me*, I remind myself. The more I can control my urges while hungry, the more it means I can walk amongst humans when I escape this hell.

Helios takes off his gloves by tugging at each fingertip until the material slips off his hands. He tosses the gloves onto his dresser and spins around to face me. He smiles then, combing a hand through golden curls.

My eyes follow the movement, just as the daylight ring on his pinky finger sparkles. Helios sits next to me on the bed. I flinch and try to hide it by standing.

"Beautiful young thing," he says, as if lost in a fond memory. "Reminded me of you, before you were turned. He had long blond hair and vibrant blue eyes. Not quite as pretty as you were, but still my type." He grins.

"Sorry I no longer please you, Helios," I bite back

as I walk toward our bedroom window. In some weird, fucked-up way, I know Helios was paying me a compliment, but I never wanted to be a vampire. Never wanted to be here.

"Aw, don't be like that." His silver eyes gleam. "You know how sexy humanity is to an immortal."

Once, Helios admitted he enjoyed seeing me jealous. Just another good reason to continue pretending. I'm always pretending around these vampires, ever since I was kidnapped at just fifteen.

A soft tapping sound comes from the door.

"I asked Nico to join us."

My stomach growls loudly and Helios chuckles. The heat returns to my face.

Helios stands to answer the door, pausing in front of me. He traces a finger over my cheeks. "I love how you can still blush, my sweet. Give it a hundred years or two, and that will go away. But for now, at least, I can pretend my young husband is still human."

It takes all my willpower not to pull away. Instead, I stare into his gaze, never breaking eye contact, as if we are equals. I used to quiver under these vampires, scared of making a wrong move. Oh, how far I've come. Sometimes I pretend to still be the meek little human they stole in the middle of the night. Though I plan and plot, moving across the imaginary board until I, a mere pawn, can take them all down.

Nico enters the room, his eyes immediately locking on mine. Excitement radiates from the handsome young witch, and hope swirls in my stomach. As soon as Helios turns his back to shut the door, Nico gives me a quiet nod.

My mind races, and I wonder if there's any way to be alone with my friend. Helios walks past me and into our bathroom. "Helios," I purr.

His head pops out of the bathroom door. He arches a brow and smirks. "Please shower. I can smell *him* on you." I narrow my eyes for good measure. "I don't want to smell your dinner while we make love later."

His smile grows even wider. "Of course, dear."

Once the water turns on, I reach for Nico's hand and tug him toward the bed eagerly. I press a finger to my lips, even though it's unnecessary. We both know we can't say anything without my husband hearing. Just in case, we both peer behind us as Helios starts singing under the shower's spray. Such a pity that someone so monstrous can possess such a pleasant voice.

Quietly, Nico pulls a cloth out of his pocket and unwraps it. My eyes widen when I see the syringe. He pulls me in close and whispers directly into my ear. "The potion only weakens and paralyzes," he says, too afraid to say anything more with a vampire so close.

I nod, taking it carefully from his hands and wrapping it back up. Tears spring to my eyes, and I mouth the words '*thank you*,' before tugging him into a fierce hug. He nods against me, trembling slightly, reminding me he's just as much a prisoner as I am.

"You must drink, Calix," he says out loud. "To keep your strength up for such an important night."

He tilts his neck in the traditional submissive pose, but I shake my head. I've always refused to drink from him like this. I know how intimate feeding can be, and I never want to force my friend to feel aroused the way I was when I was a blood slave. I reach for his wrist and bring it toward my lips.

Nico yanks his wrist back and exposes his neck again. "You'll get more this way. You need your strength. Please, drink from my neck, Calix."

A chuckle comes from the bathroom, but luckily the shower is still on. No doubt Helios heard Nico and just assumed the witch wanted to feed me... among other things. I narrow my gaze. Nico is smirking. He said it out loud because he wants Helios to hear. Nico wants me to feed. My friend is trying to help me, but I hate feeding this way. I feel like it's an act that should be done between lovers. Not friends or people who are trying to nourish me.

I frown, pulling him close to me. My fangs elongate, already eager for his blood. When I sink my teeth into my friend's throat, I make sure to push arousal through the bond—it's either that or pain. Nico immediately moans. Without preamble, I feed quickly and efficiently, then clean him up by licking the wound closed. Loud enough for Helios to hear, I tell Nico to keep his phone on and to wait for my text, as I may want to feed after my husband and I have fooled around.

Nico nods, understanding my meaning. If I can help it, I will never have to touch that vampire again after tonight. I might enjoy sex, especially when it's the only way for me to escape the boredom of being held captive. But I would prefer to have sex on my own terms, not as leverage to save my life.

When I was fifteen, a rogue vampire by the name of Dante came to my house and killed my parents. He initially took me intending to use me as a bargaining chip, but when no one came searching for either of us, he figured he would use me as a blood bag instead.

For years, rage and fear ruled my emotions. I wanted revenge, but I was too scared and fragile to take it. I was only human, after all. Back then, all vampires scared me, but shortly after being taken, I discovered only rogue vampires are the evil ones.

Fortunately, other than being held against my will and randomly treated like food, Dante wasn't necessarily mean to me. Not until I turned nineteen and someone from his nest mentioned how pretty I was. Being such a powerful figure, he realized that my beauty could gain him plenty of favor amongst the rogues living in their court. So, he showed me off like a toy, his *pretty little blood slave*. He became obsessed with me and the attention I brought him. Eventually, he passed me around to all his friends. I had to learn quickly how to harden my emotions to survive.

Terrified of being drained dry, I used my body to my advantage. A year later, I met Helios, a prince amongst the rogues. He was all power, grace, and control. The complete opposite of Dante. At first, he would request just my time, showering me with gifts and conversation before feeding from me.

Once Helios had his mind made up, he told Dante that he wanted me.

Dante refused to give me up. One night, I overheard him tell Helios the reason he killed my family. A seer told him that a Darkblade Witch would be his downfall. Helios chuckled and called Dante a fool. Helios reminded him I was still a Darkblade Witch, and that he'd gladly take me off his hands to prevent the seer's prophecy. Helios even promised to keep me captive in his mansion.

To my surprise, Dante agreed, but only if he could have one more night with me. Out of all the vampires I worried about, it turned out to be Dante who took my human life away from me. It was Dante who lost control and drained me dry. Realizing he fucked up, he turned me into a vampire before it was too late.

Helios was angry when he found me. He didn't need another vampire, but he could always use more humans to feed from. Nevertheless, he took me in and taught me how to feed. How to control my urges and deal with new abilities. At first, it was as if the prince of rogues was my savior. But after a while, Helios's true colors finally bled through. It turned out he was a monster, the same as all the other rogues.

Determined to survive, I hardened my emotions even more. I buried my fear and sorrow somewhere deep within myself. I suppressed my sadness, thoughts of my family, memories of my best friend, and any dreams I had for my once-human future. I shoved all my emotions into this tiny little treasure chest deep inside my heart and locked it away.

Then, I seduced the murderer in my bed.

I must admit, being this monster's husband is better than being a living blood bag. Dante gave me a gift the night he turned me. Not only was I no longer a blood slave, but I now had new abilities, speed, and strength. The night of my wedding to Helios, I vowed I would do everything in my power to learn how to become even stronger.

And when the time comes, I will seek revenge on those who decided to hold me against my will.

I'm dreaming of the dragon with amethyst wings, again. I used to sleep often as a human, now? Not so much. When I was trapped in that hell with Dante, I dreamt of him often—my pretty, jeweled dragon who would save me from this horrible castle. It only took me a year to realize fairytales aren't real, and I'm no princess. A dragon won't be the one to save the day. No. I need to save myself.

Cool hands wrap around my waist, and I still. My eyes snap open. Crimson curtains. Black brick walls. I'm in my room, the cold dark place that feels more like a prison than a home. Regardless, I relax when I realize it's just Helios wanting more. Always more.

I take a deep breath and count to five. It's the only amount of time I allow myself to come to terms with my situation and place my imaginary mask back in place. Prying his hands off me, I try to slide out of bed only to be stopped with a deadly grip around my neck.

Even though I'm undead, my heart rate quickens at the threat. Helios's grip tightens, and he snarls in my ear. "What did the little human mean when he said *'You must drink... To keep your strength up for such an important night.'* What's so fucking important about tonight, dear husband?"

My mind races before settling on a quick answer. "Tonight is my birthday," I snarl back.

His fingers loosen their hold. Thank the gods I'm not facing Helios, because my gaze unconsciously darts to my robe, concealing the potion that renders vampires immobile for a couple of hours.

As soon as he lets go, my inhuman vampire speed is

taking me as far away from Helios as possible. I lean against the far wall near the sliding door to our balcony. Since I moved so quickly, it caused the blackout curtains to flutter.

Helios growls. "Get away from the window, Calix. Do you want to burn yourself in the morning sun?"

"Well," I say, trying to distract him. "Aren't you going to say happy birthday?"

He grits his teeth, still on edge. I force my face to relax and give him the sultry look I've perfected over the years. "Helios, aren't you going to say happy birthday?" I repeat.

His face softens. "Happy birthday, dear. How old are you? I never keep track of such trivial things."

"Thirty."

"Right, thank the gods you can't age. Nineteen suits you. Could you imagine me trying to show off a thirty-year-old human?" He laughs.

Anger rushes through me. *Bastard*. "I was twenty when I was turned against my will," I snap. I walk to the closet door that's partially open, pull out my robe, and tuck my phone into the pocket.

He waves a hand in the air dismissively. "Don't ruin it for me, Calix. If I say you look nineteen, then you look nineteen."

I wrap the white terry cloth around my body, feeling vulnerable—another useless emotion that does nothing but hurt me.

"Take it off. I don't like it when your body is covered."

Helios has been becoming more and more impatient with me lately. Not to mention, I see the way he eyes Nico. If I'm going to escape this hell, I'll need to do it sooner rather than later. I have to run before Helios decides to just get rid of me once and for all. My hand slides into the pocket of my robe. As soon as my fingers touch the cloth that hides the potion, relief rushes through me.

"I would like my gift first," I reply.

"What the hell are you talking about?"

I roll my eyes. "My gifts. For my birthday. Please tell me you got me something." In the ten years that I've been imprisoned here, Helios has never gotten me a birthday present. The necklace around my neck is a pleasant reminder of the birthdays I used to celebrate. It's the one thing I allow myself, something from my old life that I cherish to this day.

"This is fucking ridiculou—"

"I want to see the sun," I interrupt. "That's what I want, for my gift."

Helios's eyes widen with shock.

I laugh bitterly. "Gods, your face. I don't want to commit suicide, dear husband. I just want to walk out into the sun for a minute."

His gaze drops to the daylight ring on his pinky finger.

I walk over to him and caress the cool metal with my fingertips. "Can I?"

"No." He spits the word out like a curse. "If this is some trick to run—"

"No trick. Just let me go on the balcony. I can't jump from a third-story building onto the rocks below. I can't run. I just want to feel the sun on my skin."

He studies me for a moment before he finally nods. Helios twirls the ring with his thumb. "Okay, three minutes. You walk outside, take in your fill, then you walk right back in."

My heart pounds. Holy shit, I never thought he would say yes. He tugs his ring free and holds it out to me. With trembling hands, I pluck it from his open palm. The ring fits perfectly onto my ring finger, a fact I'll find ironic later, I'm sure.

Pushing the door open, I walk out into the sun for the first time in ten years.

Sunshine sparkles on the blue lake in front of me and birds chirp in the distance. I'm hit with a sudden wave of sadness. Why did I ever take my freedom for granted? Is it possible that the dam of emotions I've suppressed for so long could really be broken by a bird's song or the warmth on my skin?

Tears flood my eyes. This isn't sympathy for my previous human existence, it's rage towards my captors. Anger for my lost future, and fury for my family, who were murdered in front of me. I stagger. Overwhelmed with emotions.

I gasp.

"The sun is beautiful, isn't it?" Helios stands by the balcony door, wrapped in shadows. I wonder if he has a special attachment to the sun because of his name, or if most vampires just crave what they can't have.

I tilt my head upwards and enjoy the warmth like a cat in the sun. After what seems like only a minute, Helios speaks up. "Time's up, Calix. Come back inside. Now."

The intensity of his demand tightens around my chest. It's as if my heart is constricted by chains. I stand there under the sunlight for a moment longer. Helios snarls. Pasting a fake smile on my face, I walk back into the room and throw my arms around his neck.

"Thank you."

His grip around me becomes dangerously tight. "Next

time, you'll listen, or you won't like it when I punish you."

The last thread of control snaps. With inhuman speed, I yank the syringe out of my pocket and plunge it into Helios's neck.

Helios reaches for me furiously, hand stretched out and almost wrapping around my throat when the potion kicks in, causing him to freeze in place.

To my shock, Helios speaks, still able to talk. "What the fuck have you done?"

I stumble back a step, lips parted, heart racing. After a minute of just standing there like a deer caught in the headlights, I finally move. The first thing I do is text Nico.

> Calix: I need you. Come to my room. ASAP.

"You foolish fucking boy. Fix me," Helios demands.

I rush back into my room and start shoving clothes into a duffle bag. Then, with shaky hands, I yank the mini fridge in the corner open and stuff a small cooler with blood bags. *Fuck. Where the hell is Nico?*

Helios is still frozen in place by the balcony door. "If you run, I'll find you. How long does this potion last?" Helios chuckles. "A few minutes? Hours? How far do you think you can get before I come after you?"

Don't listen to him. This is my only chance for freedom. I'll never have an opportunity like this again. I just want to be free. It'll be worth it when I get far away from this place. Away from these evil vampires who want to control every aspect of my life; when I eat, when I sleep, who I fuck. Soon enough, my life will be my own again.

The soft click of the door sounds behind me, and I whip around in time to see Nico take in the scene. His mouth falls open and sweat beads on his forehead.

From this angle, Helios can't see the door. "Who is that? Nico, is that you? I can smell your fear, boy. Come over here and help me."

Nico turns wide eyes my way. When his gaze sweeps over my body and to my bags, Nico visibly relaxes, looking relieved. The kind smile he gives me thaws my cold heart. It's been so long since someone seemed concerned about my well-being. I finish shoving clothes into my duffle.

"Did he hurt you?" Nico asks, lightly touching my shoulder. I shake my head.

"Nico!" Helios roars. "Get over here and help me."

The young witch looks frightened, but he's brave. Braver than I was at his age. A decade ago, I couldn't imagine myself just not responding to the furious vampire. Nico's magical bloodline allows him to fight the vampire compulsion radiating from Helios.

"Tell me what's going on. Are you both running? Together?" Helios laughs as if the mere thought is funny. "How fucking romantic." The longer we ignore Helios, the angrier he gets. There is nothing romantic between Nico and me, but something tells me Helios could never understand.

I zip the duffle closed and secure the latch on the cooler filled with blood bags.

"Both of you are going to fucking pay for this shit. Nico, you're dead. Fucking dead, you hear? I'm going to feed from you until you're dizzy and confused. Then I'm going to take that virginity you treasure so much." Despite Helios's cruel words, a moment of relief washes over me. At least they didn't take that from Nico, too.

"And you, dear husband, I know how much you hated being passed around. I saved you from that, you foolish boy. I saved you from nightly torment, and this is how you repay me?" Helios snarls. "I'm going to make you watch while I take this little witch apart. Then when I'm done with you, if you're lucky, maybe I'll return you to Dante and his friends."

Blood rushes to my head, and I feel the moment my emotionless mask crumbles to ash. Panic. Rage. Fear.

During my blind panic and all the blood rushing to my head, I don't realize that Nico's heart rate has picked up speed. It's not until I hear the whimper that tumbles from his throat do I register his fear. Helios's arm is no longer stretched out. Somehow, it's now down at his side.

I gasp.

He's breaking through the spell. If he's strong enough to move now, that means I might only have a few more minutes. Helios is talking to Nico still, trying to compel him from a distance. When that doesn't work, the threats start up again. Continuing to break through the spell even further, Helios turns his head.

Then he smiles. It's a cruel, wicked thing that promises pain and torture.

Tears pool in Nico's eyes. It's like looking into a mirror of my past self. There is so much sorrow and fear there.

"You only have two minutes, maybe three, Calix. Come here and maybe I'll forgive you. Come here and I won't hurt the little witch."

"You won't hurt him?" I ask, hearing the lie in his words.

"Come here. Drop to your knees and beg."

My head jerks up and I see it.

There's a wild, almost animalistic look in Helios's eyes.

He's excited. Turned on. A true predator, taunted by his prey.

My soul is burning with a rage so hot that I'm surprised he can't sense it. I've been a captive for too long. Stuck with these rogues for over a decade. I've been dreaming of the day a beautiful dragon will save me. Dreaming of the day when I will save myself.

I'm so fucking tired of dreaming.

The cold, constricting chains around my heart snap, and with all my inhuman speed, I rush to his side. One second, I'm by the bed, and in the blink of an eye, I'm by Helios's side, images of all the awful things he will do to us playing like a reel in my head. "All right, husband, you wanted me by your side? Here I am."

And before I can fully register my true intentions, I shove him with all my vampiric strength. He stumbles through the open balcony door and into the sunlight.

At first, nothing happens, and when his angry, bewildered eyes snap up to meet mine, I panic. I slam the door shut before he can walk back into the room. I don't know what I expected; maybe for Helios to burst into fire and scream in pain? For his body to start smoking and sizzle under the sun's rays?

Either way, I'm not prepared for the way red magic

swirls in the air and lights up around his body right before Helios turns completely black and slowly crumbles into a pile of ash.

A sob startles me out of my shock. I spin around and gather the crying witch into my arms. "Hush, now. That monster doesn't deserve any tears. We're free, Nico. We can leave. No one will ever hurt us again."

Nico embraces me tighter, as he repeatedly murmurs '*thank you*' between his sobs.

"No one will ever hurt us again," I repeat as the witch pulls away from me with a happy, watery smile.

He waves a hand through the air and chants a spell. Just outside the glass door, Helios's ashes drift away on a magical wind. Nico smiles. "Never again."

I twirl the daylight ring on my finger. For the first time in over ten years, hope swirls in my chest.

Chapter Two

ZERO

The doorbell rings. "I got it!" I call out into the house before jogging to the front door and swinging it open.

My best friend, Rook, stands in the doorway with a large bottle of expensive whiskey in his clawed hands. His wide and tall wolf body—well, partial-werewolf body—fills the doorway completely.

A giggle sounds from somewhere behind Rook, before his mate, Autumn, rushes forward and wraps me up in a brief hug.

"What are you two doing here?" I ask with a grin.

"It's not every day the world's most famous rogue vampire hunter retires and moves to our small town," Autumn says, causing me to laugh.

I wave them through the doorway. "Well, get the hell in here. Let me show you two around."

Rook whistles low, taking in the place with fresh eyes. "I never took you as the type to own a mansion. Maybe a swanky bachelor pad, but this? This is grand, even for you."

Autumn's green eyes sparkle as he winks and brushes past Rook. Since the witch is a direct descendant of Heart's Hollow's founding covens, he knows the exact length of time it took me to complete the construction of this house. And in this specific area, no less.

"Wow. This place really is huge," Autumn says as he glances around at the extravagant foyer. "I've seen it from the outside, but never realized just how spacious it is."

I nod. "Twelve bedrooms. I wanted a place big enough for my team to call home in between missions." It might seem frivolous, or too big for a single amethyst dragon, like myself. But I wanted a huge place in a safe haven town that would be here for my entire team. This might be my home, but its doors are wide open to those who have had my back for years.

Killing vampires has consumed my thoughts for about fifteen years now. Ever since my best friend and I witnessed his entire family being slaughtered in front of us. That day will forever be etched into my memory; the rogue vampire was deranged and cruel, taking joy in all the killing before kidnapping Calix. I was only seventeen, and Calix was fifteen. As soon as I became an adult and my dragon appearance surfaced, I joined the Elite Guard, eager to find the bastard who took my best friend.

After ten years of searching for and killing any rogue vampires that I could get my claws on, I had to come to terms with the likelihood that Calix was no longer alive. I saw the horrible things they did to human pets. They treated them like walking blood bags. The chances of my best friend surviving the night he was taken were very unlikely.

It was my team—my chosen family—who pulled me out of that dark place of anger and revenge. As if sensing my dark thoughts, Gideon emerges from the kitchen, a huge deli sandwich in hand. "Hey, Bossman. Who was at the door? Oh, hi—" he trails off when he spots the partially shifted wolf and powerful witch standing there.

"Gideon, this is one of my best friends, Rook. We grew up in the same paranormal town before I joined the guard. This stunning witch is Autumn, Rook's mate."

Gideon's face splits into a wide smile. "Autumn and I already met; he was the Sinclair Witch who approved of my residency before I was able to move here." Certain safe haven towns take extra pride in the safety of their residents and enforce an interview process for new residents.

Even though all safe havens have magical wards that literally push dangerous people out of town and protect the residence from people who have evil intentions, it's hard for the magic to gauge whether someone was here for shady reasons.

Case in point: last month, I had the pleasure of arresting a deceitful witch by the name of Meyer Cunningham. The witch was peddling questionable potions and had morals that were even more suspect. Not only was he shady, but some of the potions he had on hand were dangerous.

Rook sniffs the air, trying to decipher what type of paranormal creature Gideon is. My lips twitch. One of Gideon's abilities is to change his scent, making him one of the best trackers in the Elite Guard; always able to hunt down his prey without leaving a trace.

Rook holds out a hand to Gideon, and my dragon warms in my chest, happy that two of my closest friends are finally meeting. Since losing Calix at such a young age, my dragon could feel my anguish when he surfaced. While some dragons might hoard treasures, jewels, or collectibles, I hoard those I care about. Whether it's by actually accepting them into my chosen family, or something as simple as using my photography skills to photograph a special moment between us, I pride myself in making special connections with others.

Over the next thirty minutes or so, I take Rook and Autumn through my house, showing them each room, from all the bedrooms to the kitchen, dining room, game room, theater, and even the ballroom. All the while, Gideon trails behind us munching on his food and making silly comments that make us all smile.

Rook laughs as he takes in the marble floors and chandeliers. "What on earth are you going to do with a ballroom?"

I shoot him a playful grin. "Your mate's family has no issues throwing grand balls and dances. Who knows? Maybe I'll throw a few parties or maybe even a masquerade."

Autumn's eyes twinkle. "I love masquerades. If you're serious, let me know, and I can help. Maybe throwing you a huge party will make things easier for welcoming you to town."

Gideon nudges me. "Who knows, maybe you'll meet someone special."

My dragon swishes his tail at that. *Hush, you. Finding a mate is one of the main reasons we wanted to retire, remember?* He huffs in reply.

We make our way outside and toward the gardens. As Gideon and Rook walk ahead of us, Autumn lingers closer to me. I get the feeling that he and Rook planned this. I smirk at my new witch friend.

"How are you doing?" Autumn asks.

I want to arch a brow and continue smirking, but by the sound of Autumn's tone, I can tell he wants a serious answer. I'm not just looking at my friend, I'm being questioned by a Sinclair Coven member who is concerned for a fellow resident.

"I'm doing okay. I feel a little lost if I'm being honest."

Autumn nods encouragingly.

"I've been so excited to build my forever home here in Heart's Hollow, but now that it's done and I'm retired, I don't know what to do with myself."

"Well, what kind of hobbies do you have? Or what's something you would have done before you were in the Elite Guard?"

"I would take photos," I say without thought. The idea of me pulling out my professional camera springs to mind. I love photography of all kinds, but there's something soothing about viewing the world through a lens and hearing the click of the shutter. It's something I used to do with Calix, and it's something I do when trying to de-stress between missions. A sudden need to explore the town and take photos overcomes me. "Thanks, little witch."

I purse my lips, still feeling troubled.

"What else are you thinking about?"

Glancing over at Autumn, I see the concern in his eyes. Looks like I'm not hiding anything today.

"For approximately fifteen years, my thoughts have been consumed by the idea of eliminating as many evil vampires as I can find. As one of the busiest Elite members, I strive on schedules and plans. I'm always on the go. My life was fast and exhilarating. But I know, deep down, I'm bone tired. I want to find someone to fall in love with. I want what you and Rook have, but am I really ready to give it up, just like that? For someone who might not even exist?"

I blow out a deep sigh, ruffling the hair that fell across my forehead. I didn't mean to confess all that.

"Can I be honest with you?" Autumn pauses, facing me.

"Please. I could use all the help and advice possible."

"I think you're ready. You're just scared."

I bark out a laugh. "I can't remember the last time I was

scared." That's a lie. I'll never forget the fear that pulsed through my veins when that vamp took Calix from my grasp. Calix's beautiful, wide blue eyes had begged for me to help him, but the compulsion the rogue had over me kept me in place, frozen there; unable to help the person who meant the most to me.

Guilt eats away at me to this day.

Autumn shakes his head. "I'm not talking about that adrenaline-pumping fear, I'm talking about those nerves that cause you to question things. That little niggling fear making you want to cling to what you know best, so you won't have to face the future? It's *that* fear of failing."

I scoff. "Why would I be afraid of failure? Do you know how many missions I've failed since joining the Elite Guard? Zero. It's why it's my chosen dragon's name. I never had any intention of ever failing a single mission."

My dragon sits up straighter in my chest and we both puff with pride as I flex my amethyst wings. "My dragon and I have faced many evils and saved so many people."

Autumn and I resume walking. "Cocky as ever, I see." He chuckles.

"Hey, it's confidence." I wink.

Autumn tugs me to one of the viewing benches in the middle of the rose garden. "Zero, I know you're brave.

And you've done so much good for both humans and paranormals alike. But what I'm talking about is the fear of searching for someone you want to spend the rest of your life with. That fear of putting yourself out there and finding someone who will accept all of you. You once told me your dragon's biggest dream is finding your mate. But what happens if you move here only to discover you can't find anyone willing to accept your dragon or the fact that you're a vampire hunter?"

The air whooshes from my lungs and my heart pounds. My lips fall open with shock. It's as if Autumn has seen right through my soul and plucked a fear I haven't been able to fully voice. My amethyst wings tuck around me protectively. "What does that say about me? That '*Zero, the Elite Guard's Infamous Vampire Hunter*' not only wants to find love, but is afraid no one will love him? That no one will love me—"

Autumn squeezes my hand and smiles. "I think it means you're a dragon worth loving."

The next day, Autumn's words replay through my mind

as I make my way down the cobblestone sidewalks of Heart's Hollow. A chill in the air marks the beginning of the shift from fall to winter. And yet, the sun remains high in the sky, giving me the perfect amount of light for my impromptu photography session.

The strap of my DSLR camera rests on my neck, providing comfort to my already frayed emotions. As I turn the corner, the colorful shops of downtown come into view. From this angle, I can capture the perfect photo to showcase just how charming this town really is.

Click. Click. Click. Click.

I continue snapping photos of anything and everything that catches my fancy when a strange tug directs me in a specific direction. The pull feels almost magical, but not quite. Maybe more intuition, or as if my dragon is guiding me down a certain path? Only, my dragon is silent inside of me, ears perked up and just as curious as me.

We pass by Rook's Apothecary, the bakery, and the cute little café that serves my favorite pastries. I let the feeling guide me until I'm standing in front of another shop. My blood runs cold. Witchful Thinking. This is the very shop that housed all the illegal potions and dangerous charms. The same shop I had to shut down when that jerk, Meyer Cunningham, showed his true colors.

My heart pounds when the tug to go inside becomes stronger, making my first initial thought wrong. This is definitely magic. What the fuck? Did the Elite Guard miss something? I'm used to following my intuition when on a mission. An open sign catches my eye. I take a few steps back and glance up at the building's storefront. Instead of the gaudy bubblegum pink that once said 'Witchful Thinking,' there's a beautiful sign with a red script that now reads 'The Magic Shop.'

I scoff. "A little on the nose, if you ask me," I mumble to myself. Despite the name being obvious, it doesn't come across as a mockery of magic, like Meyer's shop did. And since arresting Meyer, Autumn and his coven have placed even more wards as precautions around the town. So, I don't think I'm sensing any danger. Not to mention, the coven's interviewing process is more extensive. And if that's the case, what is this magical pull telling me to go inside the shop and look for answers?

Upon entering, a pleasant scent of incense and books immediately surrounds me. Usually, my dragon senses are sensitive to different smells, but something about this scent is comforting, reminding me of home. I peer around, shocked at how different The Magic Shop is compared to the store it was just weeks ago. Somehow, the place looks even larger than it once was, with ceilings that look impossibly taller than before. Books are arranged along the walls, and leaning against the shelves are several rolling ladders.

"Why hello, young dragon. Welcome to The Magic Shop," someone calls out from behind a checkout counter.

Dressed in mostly black, is a mysterious-looking man in a top hat. His eyes are black. Almost too black, indicating he might not be human. He's clean-shaven with a medium skin tone. I can't quite tell what nationality or species he is, but my inner dragon immediately settles, sure that this man isn't a threat to us.

Something about him looks familiar, but I can't quite place where I've seen him before. Or maybe he just has one of those familiar faces? "Have we met?" I ask.

The man gives me a knowing smile, and his inky eyes almost seem to sparkle in the dim lighting. "I don't think we have crossed paths before, in this life or any other. It seems as if we are meeting for the first time."

My lips twitch, and he gives me a friendly smile.

"My name is Zero." I hold my hand out to him.

He peers at it for a moment, almost as if trying to read a hidden meaning in my gesture before he shakes it. "Please, call me The Owner."

Recognition dawns, and my wings relax on my back. There are files and files of The Owner in the Elite Guard's archives. Reports of The Magic Shop appearing out of nowhere and hundreds of articles on how The Owner always seems to help those he encounters. There are also numerous drawings of the mysterious man, since no one has been able to photograph him.

My fingers twitch, itching to reach for my camera and take a photo.

"How may I help you?"

Glancing around at the shop, I feel that magical tug again. "You know what? I'm not entirely sure. Mind if I take a peek around?"

He waves his hand at me and encourages me forward. I nod my thanks and begin to make my way through the narrow aisles, making sure to have my dragon wings tucked in close to my body so I don't knock anything over. I walk through the mythology section and pass the crystals, until I'm in the middle of the tarot and divination section.

The enchanting pull now serves as a beacon in the night, pointing me towards something in the middle of the floor like a blinking light. I can't tell what it is from here, maybe a loose page from a book, or a postcard? Either way, I can tell that the paper in the middle of the shop is what's calling to me as if my life depends on it.

As I walk forward, I lean down to grab it while slim, graceful fingers also reach for it simultaneously. I chuckle as the stranger and I pick up the card at the same time before we straighten to our full height.

All the air rushes out of my lungs, and my lips part as I gaze into the most beautiful pair of ocean-blue eyes I've ever encountered.

Inside my chest, my dragon roars one word that reverberates and echoes in my head. *No!*

No, it isn't possible. I take a step back in shock, only to have my dragon roar again.

Mate.

Chapter Three
CALIX

My eyes wander up the length of the stranger who, coincidentally, picked up the same stray tarot card I reached for. If I never experienced what it felt like to be frozen in a vampire's compulsion, unable to move, that's exactly what I would think is happening now. A familiar scent of cinnamon and cloves surrounds me, reminding me of memories once lost, and a childhood worth remembering. A scent that reminds me of home.

Since following Nico to Heart's Hollow, this is the first time I felt like I've done the right thing, that this is the place where I'm meant to be. After Helios's death, I have been burdened by lingering feelings of guilt that won't go away, no matter how many times Nico tells me I saved the both of us.

Even though I trust Heart's Hollow's wards, I can't shake the feeling that something bad is about to happen.

But as I stare up into this tall dragon's amethyst eyes, I feel… safe. He's a good half-a-foot taller than my five-foot-seven—maybe taller. Gorgeous purple and magenta scales adorn the left side of his face and trail down his neck and collarbone before disappearing into a black dress shirt. Since the shirt is rolled at the sleeves, I can see more jeweled scales on his well-defined arms.

Then there are the transparent purple wings folded against the handsome stranger's back. I'm completely captivated by his good looks, and that's saying something, since I literally spent the last half of my life surrounded by unnaturally good-looking vampires. I've heard of love at first sight, but is there such a thing as infatuation at first sight?

I swallow hard, taking in more of his appearance, including the purple claws that look dangerously sharp. Regardless of the potential danger, he's breathtaking. Is it because he is the first dragon shifter I've met in real life? Or am I transfixed because his coloring reminds me so much of the dragon I've spent years dreaming of?

"Impossible," he whispers, almost as if in awe.

"I'm so sorry," I stammer. "Is this your tarot card?"

He glances down at the card and blinks. The card is beautiful, with a black background that's dotted with silver stars and symbols. An angel is in the center of the card with his wings spread wide. His hands are positioned casually in front of him, loosely open, palms up. Below the angel are several open coffins with spirits rising out, arms outstretched.

Both the dragon shifter and I are still grasping the card, and I wonder if he also feels the need to hold on, just like I do.

"Ah, the judgment card," The Owner says suddenly, causing both the dragon and me to jump. He hovers his hand just above the card and looks like he is reaching for it when he yanks his hand back, almost as if it's hot to the touch and he doesn't want to get burned.

The dragon's curious eyes meet mine before we return our attention back to the mysterious man in the top hat.

"Interesting," The Owner hums.

I arch a brow. "What's interesting?" I glance back down at the card as if it holds all the answers to the universe.

"It appears there's no need for me to provide a tarot reading for either of you; the card has chosen."

Okay, because that isn't ominous or slightly creepy. "It chose me?" I ask in shock. And what the hell did that mean? How can a card just choose someone?

The Owner nods, and the dragon next to me relaxes.

"And you as well, young dragon. The card has chosen both of you."

"Zero," he corrects. "My name is Zero. So what does the judgment card represent? Is it about letting go of certain prejudices? Because trust me, I'm hearing the message more often than not these days." His tone is serious, which surprises me.

Earlier, I noticed Zero when he walked into the shop. He was charming, with a lightness to him I envied. Even when he bumped into me, he was chuckling. I used to be so lighthearted and jovial. I feel like I'm slowly becoming that person again now that I'm free, but I'm not quite there, and I hate it. I hate what the rogues took from me.

"Not exactly," The Owner says. He waves a hand at a nearby table, indicating that we take a seat. "Did either of you walk into my store searching for something specific?"

I let go of the card and sit in front of the table.

Zero shakes his head and takes a seat next to me. "I'm not looking for anything." He scoots in close, and I feel his thigh brush up against mine. Heat zaps through my body. Did he do that on purpose? I turn my head to offer him a small smile, but he's already focused on The Owner.

"And what about you?" The Owner looks at me as he takes a seat across the table and pushes aside a crystal ball.

He pulls out a pretty wood box of tarot cards, shuffles the deck, and flips a card before sliding it in front of us. I don't need to look down to know it's also the judgment card.

I bite my lip, a little nervous to admit anything out loud, but I do anyway. "No, nothing specific. I just felt like I needed to walk into the shop for some reason. Almost as if something was guiding me here."

Zero's head snaps up. His gaze is intense as he studies me for a moment. "That's what it felt like for me, too. Like a magical tug pulling me into the shop."

I nod. A magical tug. That's a good way of putting it.

The Owner gives us a knowing smile, his black eyes glittering. "Almost like a true calling, one you couldn't ignore?"

Zero and I make eye contact again.

"This card isn't exactly as it seems. Judgment is an exciting card to pull. It's all about rebirth, an inner calling, or a true calling, if you will. For many, it represents a new chapter in your life, or in some cases, reinventing your life."

My heart pounds even more as The Owner begins to explain things like the meaning of absolution and starting over. He explains that life *'before'* might have had limitations, or restraints holding one back. This card is all about embracing that new life now that we are free. As he talks, I find myself completely absorbed in his explanation. The Owner must be talking about me.

It makes sense. The rogues have literally held me captive for years. Now that I'm free, I should be embracing my new life here in Heart's Hollow. It's about reinventing myself. The way The Owner emphasizes certain words and looks right at me, it's as if he's staring into my soul. This explanation is too specific to *not* be me. Right?

I glance back over at Zero, but like me, he's leaning forward, listening to every word the mysterious man tells us. Maybe he's entering a new chapter in his life, too?

"That's the light side of the card. An explanation if someone is to pull the card in the upright position. But like everything else, there's always the reverse."

My heart drops. "The reverse, as in the opposite?"

Zero unconsciously reaches over and grasps my hand. Is he trying to comfort me? I lace my fingers with his, basking in the warmth this dragon is providing me.

"If you were to pull the reverse, it can mean one of you has a lot of self-doubt. Your inner critic might be pushing you to ignore the call. But really, how can one fully ignore a soul's true calling once awakened to it?"

My mind scrambles as I look down at the new card on

the table. It's sitting beside the original card that Zero and I found on the ground. Did I reach for it in the upright position, or was it upside down? I can't remember. And if I got the card in the upright position, does that mean Zero pulled the reverse?

Zero stands abruptly, his chair toppling over with a loud crash. "I'm sorry. I need to go." Without further explanation, he places the chair back in the upright position and storms out of the shop. As the shop's front door swings shut, I look down at the table and realize he has taken the original tarot card with him.

The Owner smiles. "Don't worry, Calix. He'll come back around." He hands me the other remaining judgment card, and I take it. It isn't until I'm down the street do I realize I never gave The Owner my name.

I make my way down the cobblestone path that leads me to the big gazebo in the park. The first time I saw the white wood covered in vibrant green vines and dangling purple wisteria, I had to stop and just appreciate its beauty.

From here, I can see Autumn sparking purple magic

into the plants while his little fox familiar plays in a pile of fallen leaves a few feet away.

A moment of deep sorrow hits me. I used to be a witch, just like Autumn. I remember Autumn from when I was a child. Both of us grew up in prominent witch families. Both of us were important members of our coven. The day Dante turned me into a vampire was the day my coven's magic within me died.

Autumn glances up and waves me over. Shaking off my emotions, I think back at what The Owner told me. This is me embracing my new life, a new chapter that I plan to fill with happiness. To my shock, Autumn hugs me when I reach his side.

"Thanks for meeting with me," I say as I hug him back.

"No problem. My mate is happy to help. Rook is an expert at potion brewing." He hands me a small vial with a swirling red liquid inside. "Are you sure you want to drink it? The point of being in a safe haven town is to be accepted, no matter what species you are."

I nod. "I'm sure. I don't want others to realize I'm a vampire, at least not until my new home is secured within the town's borders." I'm just grateful that the last potion I took is still hiding my vampire nature from everyone.

"No, you're right. It's smart," Autumn agrees. "I

promise, I'm working hard with the coven to expand the town's limits along with the wards. I know you wanted a location at the edge of the forest so you can hunt animals for blood."

"You don't need to say the word '*hunt*.' I prefer saying '*feed from animals*,' since I don't plan on hurting them."

"Of course. I should have asked. I'm so sorry."

I wave his apology away and squeeze his arm. "It's okay, you didn't know. Plus, I'm pretty sure it's just a 'me thing.'"

"Just in case you need it, I'm looking into how I can get regular blood bags donated. I know vampires can't just survive on small animals."

"Thank you, Autumn. It's been a long time since I've felt welcome anywhere."

The day Nico and I entered Heart's Hollow, I was shocked to find out that the wards would accept me, a vampire who had just killed someone. When we started the resident's interview to see if we could be accepted into the town, I ended up confessing everything to Autumn. I don't know if it was the truth serum at work, but I get the feeling I wanted to tell Autumn either way.

I didn't want my history creeping up on me. If I needed to go into hiding, I wanted to know sooner rather than later. Once he heard my whole story, he reassured me I was meant to be in this town.

Autumn and I start chatting about everything and nothing as he continues to nourish the plants with his magic. He talks to me about the town, his coven, and eventually, the topic moves over to his wolfy mate, Rook. It's obvious the witch is in love, and rightfully so. If I'm being honest, I have to admit that I'm jealous. No one has ever treated me the way Autumn talks about his fated mate.

While Autumn recounts how he and Rook met, I twist the cap off the bottle of my potion and down it in one go. The liquid feels cool as it slides down my throat, but I'm shocked by its delicious apple taste. Autumn and I continue talking. We reminisce about a few memories of when we were little and our families met. Then he walks me to the edge of the forest.

"Text or call if you need anything."

I rush forward and hug Autumn, thankful to have met another friend. "Thank you for being so kind and helping me out. It means the world to me that you not only accepted me into your town, but you're working with the coven to include my new place within the town's limits."

We say our goodbyes and I walk leisurely through the

forest. I take my time, admiring the trees, the blue sky, and the sun above me. Unconsciously, I toy with the daylight ring on my finger as my thoughts stray to the sexy dragon I met earlier. What was it about him?

The whole time Autumn recounted stories of his mate, my mind kept conjuring up images of Zero and how I wished he were there with me. Strange. I don't think I've ever had a crush before.

Then, when Autumn told me he and Rook have shared dreams, a sign that they are, in fact, fated mates, memories of an amethyst dragon came to mind. Sure, the dragon in my dreams was a fully shifted dragon, as big as a van, and not the mysterious stranger I met at The Magic Shop. But one can wish.

I'm lost in silly daydreams with a small smile on my face to distract me, that I don't notice at first that the door to my new house is wide open.

The blood drains from my face, and I feel dizzy as I look at the open door. This place isn't protected by Heart's Hollow's wards just yet, but I thought I would be safe, hidden in this forest. Adrenaline pumps through me as I spot the shattered glass of my window. It looks as if the person broke through my window and reached the lock just inside the door.

I cock my head and listen, using my vampire abilities to listen for another heartbeat. Nothing. I'm alone, with the exception of some birds chirping in the distance. I step into my house and feel the stupid tears flood my eyes as I take in the chaos. Things are broken and ripped to shreds. Everything is haphazardly thrown around.

Nothing in this house actually meant anything to me, since it's all new, but still. This was my place. My new home. The new chapter I was excited to start. As I glance around at all the broken things, it dawns on me. This was done with purpose. Either one of Helios's friends or one of his many lovers. Fuck, it might even be one of his enemies, assuming I'll take care of my husband's debt, or some such bullshit.

Fear starts creeping in before I squash it away, pushing it aside to make room for fury. Screw that. No more. I told myself that once I was free, I wouldn't fear anyone else, and I want to hold true to that vow. Pulling out my phone, I text Autumn and pray that he meant it when he said I can ask for anything.

Chapter Four
Zero

A DEAFENING SILENCE FILLS the shop. I blink. Did my best friend's mate just say what I thought he did? Rook places a mug of hot tea in front of me and I instantly recognize the calming brew. Like fucking hell am I going to calm down.

"What the hell do you mean, you need me to protect a vampire?" Over the course of the last fifteen years, since joining the Elite Guard, not once have I been asked to protect the very creature I've been trained to hunt down.

Rook pushes the tea even closer to me before taking a seat at the small table. "You said you'd be mature about this," my best friend grumbles.

The three of us are in Rook's Apothecary. Autumn called me, sounding frantic and in need of a huge favor. I peer over at Autumn. He's chewing on his lip nervously as he stares at me. "He's a friend," Autumn says, as if that's explanation enough. I roll my hand in the please continue gesture. "He's a good person. He passed through Heart's Hollow's wards, has been interviewed and even drank a truth serum. He passes all our tests, even a few of my own."

"Well, that piece of shit, Meyer, passed through the wards too," I reply lamely.

"You know the coven and I have improved the spells and charms since. And like I said, he passed numerous tests, ones we've added since Meyer was arrested."

"Then tell me why he needs protection, if he's so damn innocent," I snap.

Rook sighs. "Drink the damn tea I made before it gets cold."

I narrow my eyes at my friend. "You didn't add something else to it, did you, potions master?" I meant it as a joke, but as soon as the words leave my mouth, I know I made a mistake.

Rook slams his fist on the table, causing my tea to slosh. Then he stands and walks into the back room of his shop. My eyes widen. I don't think I've ever seen Rook furious before. Not like that. I start to stand, but Autumn places a hand on my forearm.

"Let him cool down. Zero, he'll be here any minute. I

need your help. It isn't my story to tell, and I want him to tell it to you. You're the professional."

All the fight leaves me in a whoosh. I pick up the calming tea and drink the warm liquid in two swallows. An explosion of flavor coats my tongue and my nerves instantly soothe. "Fuck, that's good. Who needs alcohol when you can have this on hand? It's natural and gets the job done. Yes, please."

Autumn chuckles. "You know that tea only works on dragons."

I smile. "True. Now, tell me why, when I have a house with three other team members and hopefully more before the end of the year, did you choose the vampire hunter to protect your friend?"

"You're the one I trust, Zero. I trust you with my life."

"Ah shit, kid." I rub my chest, unable to fight my smile from growing wider. "You know how to punch a dragon in his feels."

Autumn shakes his head, but I don't miss the way his lips twitch at the corners. "Plus, you're the only retired one. What if one of your teammates gets called in for a mission? I don't want my friend abandoned."

I blow out a deep sigh and try to swallow another swig from my empty mug. I might be calm, but my dragon is still aggravated inside of me. "All right, I'll hear the vamp out. But I'm not making any promises. I'm going to step outside real quick and get some air. Text me when the vampire has arrived."

The little witch hops up and throws his arms around me. "I knew I could count on you."

Something soft brushes against my leg, and I see Maple, Autumn's fox familiar, cooing as she brushes against me. Despite my hesitance, my dragon and I puff with pride. '*Family,*' my dragon says down through our bond.

Once I'm outside, I make my way to the side of the building and lean against the brick wall. Deep down, I know not every vampire is bad. Hell, I've met several decent vampires, but when I'm around one, my brain goes into hyperdrive. I want to interrogate them, ask them if they happen to know the vampire who took my childhood friend away from me. Even now, my fingers itch to grab one of the photos I have in my wallet for such an occasion.

I have so many photos of my friend. I wasn't kidding when I mentioned my hoard was filled with photos of those I care about. I'm just thankful I got into photography when Calix was still alive, and I'm even more grateful I took the photos of him on my digital camera.

Paranoid bastard that I am, I have his photos saved in numerous places.

This could be the new chapter in my life that I need to embrace now that I'm retired. My true calling. I scoff. Not that my true calling is to protect this lone vampire. But I've already spoken with the council and with Autumn's coven. Once the town borders and wards are expanded, I want to open a safe house. A place for paranormals and humans who need protection from rogues. At least until they feel safe enough to venture out on their own. Perhaps I can start with this vampire and help protect him from whatever evils that are after him.

Maybe then, when I'm worthy enough to be called someone's mate, I can approach the pretty blond I met at The Magic Shop.

My inner dragon swirls in my chest, huffing smoke, and whipping his tail. *Easy boy. We can't be sure that stunning creature was actually our mate.* But even as the thought comes to mind, it's followed by a sense of hope.

Honestly, I think my dragon is just eager. He's been wanting a mate for even longer than I have.

"Zero? I thought that was you," a musical voice says behind me. I whip around. How did someone approach without me hearing them? Time itself comes to a halt.

As if I summoned him from out of nowhere, the pretty blond man is standing several feet away. "I'm sorry. Did I scare you?"

He's even prettier today than he was yesterday. His golden blond hair tumbles down in waves. The color framing his face makes his eyes look even more blue. I shake my head as my dragon twirls with joy. My hand wanders up to my chest and I rub small circles there, trying to calm the beast inside.

His gaze follows the motion, and he takes a step back, looking hurt. He spins on his heel.

"No, wait. Don't go." *Mate. Mate. Mate.* My dragon continues to chant, and I force myself to ignore him for the time being. I say the only thing that comes to mind. "I'm sorry I ran off yesterday."

He pauses. Slowly, he spins back around to face me.

I give him a sheepish smile. "Even dragons can't be fearless all the time."

He smiles back, and I'm once again struck by his beauty. He smirks, a playful tilt to his lips that has my cock jerking behind the zipper of my pants. "You know, I thought it was a little cliché."

I arch a brow in question.

"Your timing." He takes a few steps forward. "The

Owner asks how someone can ignore their soul's true calling, and you take that moment to literally run away?"

I bark out a laugh, not expecting such sarcasm. *I like it.* "I didn't actually run."

"I got to witness someone run away from his destiny. I guess I've seen it all," he jokes.

Closing the distance between us, I take a few steps forward. "Seen it all, huh?" I ask in a flirty tone. "Have you ever seen an amethyst dragon shift into his full dragon form?"

His eyes darken. I replay my words in my head and realize how I came across. And this pretty little thing likes it. Suddenly, I'm hard. What is it about this blond stranger that has both my dragon and me reacting so easily?

"Are you offering to show me?" He bites his lip.

Fuck, even I can hear the sexual innuendo in his melodic voice.

"Oh, there you are." Autumn is standing on the sidewalk several feet away, peering at us between the two of us. "So, you two have met?"

"Kind of." I grin at the stunning blond, internally chuckling as I realize I can't keep referring to him by his hair color. "Actually, I haven't caught your name."

That devastating smile is back as he holds out his hand for me to shake. My inner dragon pushes me forward, eager to touch skin-to-skin.

"Calix. My name is Calix Darkblade."

"Calix is the vampire I was hoping you could protect," Autumn replies at the same time.

For what feels like the millionth time in less than a week, I'm frozen in place. I'm struck stupid with shock as I stare at the beautiful stranger in front of me. Calix's hand falls to his side, and I'm vaguely aware of the conversation that's taking place between Calix and Autumn, because Calix is all I can see as the past and present start to blend together.

The down tilt to those plush lips when he frowns, a familiar narrowing of his eyes when he's suspicious, and the depth of emotion in those ocean-blue eyes. This is *my* Calix. My childhood friend I've dedicated the last fifteen years to seeking revenge for.

My Calix.

A vampire.

Chapter Five
CALIX

Horror floods me as my hand drops to my side and I realize who this dragon is in front of me. He doesn't even bother to shake my hand. He just stares at me in pure horror. It's as if tiny little puzzle pieces fall into place.

This is Zero.

I knew his name sounded familiar. The Elite Guard's infamous rogue vampire hunter. Zero, the dragon who hates vampires so much that most of the rogues just refer to him as The Vampire Slayer.

My head whips toward Autumn, betrayal filling my chest. "Do you want to explain to me why I would let a vampire hunter protect me?"

Autumn's mouth falls open. "I'm so sorry, Calix. I promise you can trust him. He only hunted rogues—"

Autumn is cut off by a pained, startling noise that

comes from Zero. It's a cry of anguish and devastation. A sound that burrows deep into my soul, calling to all the pain I've dealt with in my life. Something is wrong.

He steps forward, hand extended. His amethyst-colored eyes change from round pupils to dragon slits. His familiar cinnamon scent surrounds me. Zero's scales ripple across his arm and spread. He's fighting his shift.

My forehead creases. What the hell is going on? Fighting a shift like this is very painful. He needs to calm down.

"Calix?" Zero falls to his knees. "Is it really you?"

My eyes widen and my lip quivers. "You know me?" I study his face intently, trying to connect this handsome broken man to someone from my past. But it's been fifteen years, and I have never met a dragon before. He doesn't look familiar.

Zero's scales ripple again. Fuck. He's still fighting the shift. No matter who this person is, I need to calm him and his dragon down. The narrow space between buildings is too small for him to shift. I drop to my knees and stare at him directly in the eyes. "Hey, hey, Zero. It's okay. I need you to breathe. Look at me."

I offer him a small smile. "That's it. Look at me."

His gaze drops to my lips. His pupils shift, becoming round and more human.

Leaning forward, I hope I'm not making a huge mistake by touching this vampire hunter. Slowly, carefully, I wrap my arms around his neck. He stills, then, before I can pull away, Zero yanks me closer, pulling our bodies flush.

The hard press of his muscles against my body causes my vampire fangs to elongate. I once heard that dragon's blood is like a vampire's ambrosia. I shove those thoughts away. Zero buries his nose into my neck and breathes me in. To my shock, he licks my throat, one small claiming lick that's gone so quickly I almost wonder if I imagined it.

As he continues to hold me, I whisper sweet nothings into the air between us. Zero starts calming down in my hold, but I don't dare let go. I don't know what set this dragon off, but he seemed devastated. Distraught.

I vaguely hear Autumn say he's going to run inside and get Rook, but I don't really pay attention. My sole focus is on the trembling dragon shifter in my arms. My hand instinctively trails up to the back of his head, where I run my fingers through his hair. It's a unique color, pearl white with amethyst highlights. My thoughts briefly stray to the amethyst dragon from my dreams. Could he possibly be the same dragon? Is that how he knows me?

Maybe he isn't someone from my past, but the beast I dreamt about?

If that's the case, then I know this dragon has spent over a decade searching for me. If it was all real, and not some silly images my brain conjured up to cope with being kidnapped...if Zero is the paranormal creature from my dreams, that can only mean one thing.

Zero is my fated mate.

Chapter Six
ZERO

I SLOWLY BLINK MY eyes, taking in my surroundings, and recognize that I'm in my bedroom.

How did I even get here? Even though my bed is warm—maybe too warm—I feel surprisingly more rested than I have in a long time. Someone stirs against my back, and I go still. I'm being spooned from behind and there are slim arms wrapped around me. Clearly, the person behind me is smaller than me. Am I still dreaming? I don't even remember finding someone, let alone taking them back home.

Memories slam into me.

Autumn's request for me to protect a vampire. No, not just any vampire.

Calix. Calix. Calix.

My mate. *Our mate.*

Then I remember my reaction, and my stomach roils.

The gut-wrenching sobs, the way I fell apart. Fifteen years of holding in all that pain, anger, and grief. So much grief. And the guilt. It was too much.

My Calix has been walking this earth all this time. He isn't dead. He's here, and he's in danger.

I spin around in his arms and am met with beautiful blue eyes. Eyes that promise me the world. A future. The thoughts are whimsical and ridiculous, but then Calix's lips tilt into a smile, and I know they're true. He reaches out, trailing slender fingers across my cheekbone before he brushes the hair out of my face. We don't say a word, and at this moment we don't need to. By the way he's looking at me, he has to know we are mates.

But does he remember me? Has he thought of me at all since he was taken? I squash the thought. How selfish can I be? I don't know what Calix has been through, what kind of torture he's had inflicted on him, and that knowledge is almost as devastating as the thought of him dying that night fifteen years ago.

"What's wrong?" he asks as he sits up and flips on the lamp next to him. He's fully clothed, in a white shirt and a pair of jeans.

"How long was I out of it?"

He studies me for a moment, his blue eyes intense and

questioning. I think he knows I wanted to say something else. "A little over six hours now," he replies.

Shock reverberates through me, the warmth on my back a reminder of the way he curled against me. "And you stayed with me the whole time?"

"I did."

"But why?" I lean forward, silently begging him to understand. To recognize me as the friend he once cared for. Something catches my eye, and I glance over at the mirror above my dresser. My scales glimmer in the light. Of course, he won't remember me. When we were friends, we both thought I was a human.

Since my parents died when I was little, I never discovered my dragon heritage until my late teens, and even then, I needed to keep it a secret since dragon blood was considered very rare.

"I stayed because you are my mate," he says simply.

While my inner dragon roars with joy, disappointment hits me. I don't know why I want him to remember me so badly. Maybe because I've spent most of my life dedicated to him?

A knock sounds at my door. "Hey, Bossman. You in there?" Gideon calls out. "Silver and I just got home, and we're about to eat downstairs if you want to join us.

Lyla and Ruby stopped by and dropped off a boatload of food."

Calix arches a brow. "Lyla is Rook's sister, and Ruby is Lyla's girlfriend. Rook probably told them that my dragon would need to eat as soon as I came to. Gideon and Silver are my teammates."

Calix squeezes my hand, and I squeeze his back.

"Yeah, be down there in a minute," I call out. "I have a guest here with me. Someone I need to introduce you to."

Silence falls before I hear a low chuckle, followed by footsteps descending the stairs.

Odd.

Calix laughs. "You know you just implied we were having sex in here, right?"

I choke. "I what?" I quickly replay the words I said out loud. "Oh." My team is used to my player ways, but I need to make it very clear Calix is my mate. He's someone special, not someone meaningless. Calix has been and will always be my world. Fate made sure of that.

Calix gets out of bed and eyes my naked torso—I must have ripped it off me in my sleep. "That's okay," he teases, a sexy smirk on his face. "They can think that we had sex in here. I don't mind."

My lips twitch. Usually, I'm the flirty one in the room.

This is new. The Calix I once knew was very soft-spoken and shy. This Calix? Gods, he's all sass and dominance. This Calix is a temptation on a golden platter. I get the sneaky feeling I've met my match.

"Let me get this straight," Silver says as he sips his wine. "Autumn and Rook asked you to watch over a vampire? *You*. They know what you did for a living, right?"

Gideon, Silver, and I are sitting in the dining room, waiting for Calix to join us. He had to make a quick phone call, but I have a feeling he was giving me time to tell my team about us. I quickly explained how Autumn asked for a favor, and that when I got there, I found out it was Calix I had to protect.

Gideon narrows his eyes. "And suddenly, this vamp that you just met is upstairs in your bedroom? This doesn't sound like you—"

"Yeah, well, the guy you sound like you're describing is a prick. I don't have anything against vampires, just rogues," I snap.

Silver arches a brow. Fucking Fae. He can probably

smell the lie on me. My face heats up. Calix can probably hear everything they're saying, since they have such excellent hearing.

I throw my hands up in surrender. "Okay, okay. That guy you're describing sounds like me. The old me," I correct. "I'm going to try my hardest to embrace this new chapter in my life."

Gideon studies me. "What's changed?"

"Calix is my fated mate," I whisper. I repeat it louder. "Calix is my mate."

"Wait, Calix," Silver says. "Why does that name sound so familiar?"

Gideon's mouth drops open. "Calix, as in the Calix who—"

Calix appears at the door frame, forehead scrunched, looking confused. His wavy golden hair is loose around his shoulders. He looks so different from the kid I used to know. Back then, Calix's hair was short. Despite his lanky, slim frame, he had these adorably chubby cheeks. Now, he's still slim, but with sculpted muscles. His face has gorgeous angles and high cheekbones.

He's breathtaking.

"Hey," I say, jumping to my feet.

Calix bites his lip. He turns his attention toward Silver

and Gideon. "Hey, guys. It's nice to meet you, but do you mind if I chat with Zero alone? As he said, we're fated, but we only just met. And I'd like to get to know my mate."

Gideon gives me a questioning look. He knows all about Calix and how he was taken from me. He knows Calix is the main reason I joined the Elite Guard and became a rogue vampire hunter. As my friend stares at me, I don't know whether to nod, indicating that yes, this Calix is *my Calix*. Or if I should shake my head, silently pleading that he doesn't say a word.

Calix must see the turmoil in my eyes, because he saunters up to me, hips swaying in a seductive pull. Once he's directly in front of me, he holds out his hand. "Come, dragon. You have several things to explain to me." His tone is commanding, laced with a sensual undertone that has me growing hard in my pants. I lace his fingers with mine, feeling somehow settled yet also insanely turned on.

Holy shit, is this what it feels like to have a fated mate?

Without saying a word, I let my vampire guide me by the hand and out of the room. Behind me, Silver whispers to Gideon. "Well, fuck me. That was *hot*."

My eyes pop up to Calix's face. There's a knowing little smirk playing on his lips.

Chapter Seven

CALIX

The warmth of Zero's hand in mine is comforting. I lead him into the kitchen and gawk at all the food on the counters. It's enough to feed an entire party of people. Zero lets go of my hand and walks over to the fridge. He starts rummaging around with a cute little scrunch of the nose on his handsome face.

I start piling food onto a dish for us. Since I'm still considered a young vampire, food is still tasty to me. It might not nourish me the way blood does, but it's something I still enjoy. Since we plan on talking, I reach for finger foods that won't require a lot of attention: cubes of cheese, sliced meat, grapes, and strawberries.

Zero sighs.

"What are you looking for?" I laugh. "There's a literal buffet on the counter. Your teammate wasn't joking when he said your friends brought a lot of food."

"Lyla and Ruby had everything dropped off. You'll meet them soon. Like I said, Lyla is Rook's sister. She works at the shop with Rook. You'll also get to meet Blaze and Cass. Both work at Rook's Apothecary as well."

I nod, trying to keep all the names straight.

He pushes the fridge door closed and spots something behind me. Zero gives me a flirty grin before brushing past me and making his way to a blue cooler at the end of the counter. "Here it is. I knew they wouldn't forget you." To my shock, he reaches inside and pulls out a blood bag.

My eyes widen. "That's for me?" I can't believe his friends thought to bring me something. A warmth starts spreading throughout my chest. It's been a long time since someone did something to help me. Well, with the exception of Nico, anyway. It was as if the world around me never really cared for my well-being. My gaze bounces back up to the dragon shifter in front of me.

He chuckles. "You're the only vampire I've ever let into my home. Of course it's for you. Gods, who would have thought I would have a vampire in my house, let alone be handing him blood?"

Zero passes me the blood bag before he reaches into the cabinet behind me and hands me a wineglass. I could just bite the bag, but that's a little messy, and I appreciate the thought.

"Do you need to heat it?" He points at the bag.

"No. Despite all the movies, vampires can drink warm or cold blood. As long as it's not spoiled."

He wrinkles his nose.

I continue to place finger food on my plate. He studies my food for a moment, lost in thought. Is he already questioning things? I mean seriously, why the hell did Fate pair us together? Zero with a vampire? Even his teammates were concerned.

"How is this going to work?" I ask, placing my plate down on the counter next to my blood bag and wineglass. Zero walks right up to me and leans on the counter. Feeling suddenly vulnerable, I lower my gaze and focus on the purple-and-magenta dragon scales on his arm. The scales are stunning as they shift and glimmer in the light.

"How's what going to work?"

"Us," I whisper, still unable to look him in the face. "I'm a vampire. You hate vampires."

A deep sigh leaves Zero's nose, and I briefly wonder if he can breathe fire in his dragon form. Zero pushes away from the counter and stands in front of me. He places two fingers under my chin and tips my face up. "Calix, look at me."

Our eyes meet. His amethyst eyes swirl with an emotion I don't quite understand.

He looks at me like I mean something to him, and I tremble under his touch. I haven't meant something to someone in a long time. I know we're fated mates, and I know some mates have that whole insta-love thing happening for them. But that isn't us. That can't be us. I'm the very creature he hates.

He sighs again. His claw-tipped fingers rub my arms in a soothing up-and-down motion. "Okay. Clearly, we need to talk. There are some things I need to explain."

A nervous laugh tumbles out of me. "Gods, the whole *'we need to talk'* line. Nothing good ever follows it," I joke.

Zero continues to rub my arms as he gazes down at me with an intense look on his face. With one hand, he takes the pad of his thumb and runs it across my bottom lip. "Talking between us will never be a bad thing. If we are open and honest in our communication, our relationship has the potential to be absolutely incredible."

Our relationship.

Gods. How is this my life? When I was held captive in Helios's manor, I relied on my stories and imagination. I would weave romances in my head. Stories of strangers being fated. Soulmates reuniting. Most of the stories I wrote were insta-love.

Eventually, Nico discovered my little hobby and read one. He convinced me to publish my work. We set up my pen name and linked it to his bank account. At first, the money I earned came in slowly. We saved up for years, hiding the money from Helios as we hatched a plan to escape. One thing my readers either loved or hated was the instant connection between my characters. I would just scoff. They obviously didn't understand the power of a soulmate.

And yet, now that I'm here facing a mate of my own, I'm afraid. I'm terrified this powerful dragon in front of me might not be able to flip a switch from vampire hunter to soulmate, just like that. He says that our relationship has the potential to be absolutely incredible, and I want to believe him. But everything feels too good to be true. How can Zero already be looking at me like I'm the full moon in his night sky?

Chapter Eight

CALIX

"Follow me." Zero gathers the food, a bottle of wine and the wineglasses on the counter. I scoop up my blood bag and follow him upstairs and back to his bedroom. I half expect him to guide me to his bed. Instead, he walks over to colorful pillows and cushions in front of the large window.

Smiling, I join him at the window and peer outside. "I've always wanted a setup like this." I lounge back against the soft pillows. The view of the ocean below is beautiful. Waves crash against sand and the water sparkles in the sunlight. I close my eyes and bask in the warmth of its rays. Just a few months ago, I thought I'd never be able to see the sunlight glittering on the ocean ever again.

"I remember," Zero says, voice soft. "You wanted a huge house on the ocean and a reading nook with colorful cushions—teal, magenta, and gold, if I'm not mistaken—because you wanted a place to read or write your stories in luxury."

My eyes snap open and I sit up straight. My eyes slowly drop to the pillows that are, in fact, teal, magenta, and gold. "How did you know that? The only person who knew that was—" My voice trails off as I take in Zero's appearance again. The dragon shifter is sitting up too, eyes imploring.

"Rune?" I whisper, suddenly wishing more than anything that this is my childhood friend in front of me.

He closes his eyes and a sweet smile tips onto his lips. Fangs, similar to mine, only shorter, touch his bottom lip. He tilts his head back, reminding me of a cat sunbathing. "It's been almost fifteen years since anyone has said my human name."

"Rune," I say again, this time a little louder. "Is it really you?"

His eyes open, and I see the bright amethyst coloring, the dragon slits of his pupils, and the scales that adorn his face. How is it possible? The Rune I knew was blond. He had hazel eyes and round ears. The dragon shifter in front of me has white hair, iridescent amethyst wings, and sharp points to his pierced ears.

Then I take a closer look. Same hairstyle—even if the

color is different. The straight nose has a strong bridge. Thick arched brows, that are shaped just so. And those lips. Gods, those lips. I've had so many dreams about those lips. He must notice something in my gaze because his smile is wide and vibrant, showcasing one lone, sexy dimple. A dimple I recognize.

I gasp. "It's you. Holy shit. It's really you!" Without thinking, I throw myself across his body and into his arms. He wraps me up easily, hugging me back. My lips are quivering as tears spill down my cheeks. "Rune. Oh gods, you're a dragon? How?"

His eyes close, and then he squeezes me tight, pressing his body close. The strength of his embrace steals my breath. My head rests against his chest, and the sound of his racing heartbeat makes me feel alive.

Slowly, I pry myself off him, already missing his warmth. Red splotches of color dust his cheeks. "My dragon appeared shortly after…my eighteenth birthday."

The overhead light casts a golden glow over his skin and causes his scales to shimmer when he moves. I trace a finger across a scale just inside his wrist. "These scales suit you, pretty dragon."

A groan escapes his lips, and he blinks before flashing me a wolfish grin.

"Ah. There's the flirty Rune I remember. Would you prefer for me to call you Zero or Rune?"

"Either. But only you can call me Rune. After my dragon appeared, I found out it's tradition for dragon shifters to rename themselves. We choose a dragon name and wear it with pride."

"Zero it is, then." I smile. "I like it."

Zero's eyes flash into slits. "My dragon likes our name on your lips," he rumbles, his voice deep.

Settling back against the cushions, Zero tells me about his dragon and his shifter abilities. He pours my blood into the wineglass, and we munch on our cheese and grapes while I get reacquainted with my childhood best friend.

I let him know that I have been having dreams about his dragon for years, and his dragon confirms that we've been sharing dreams. A fact that causes him to get angry, since it could have been the key to finding me earlier. Learning that he could locate me at any time was a major shock, as he had originally joined the Elite Guard for better resources to continue searching for me.

As much as I would have preferred to be rescued, I assured Zero I was meant to stay so I could help rescue Nico.

"You've always had a kind heart," he smiles.

"Not always," I confess, guilt swirling in my stomach. "I killed my husband."

Zero growls a deep thundering sound. "Don't call him that. That vampire was your captor."

I squeeze his hand. "Sorry. It's habit now. He didn't want me calling him anything else."

"Regardless, you did what you had to. You were protecting yourself and saved your friend as well. You also prevented that bastard from doing the same thing to someone else." He places a light kiss on my temple.

How can a touch so small and sweet feel so monumental?

"Thank you," I whisper. Desire pulses between us, but I push it down. Instead, I bask in Zero's affection. I've waited fifteen years to be with this man, so I can wait a little longer.

When I finish the blood, Zero pours me a glass of Cabernet Sauvignon, and we continue to talk. As the sun sets and the sky grows dark, I realize how much I've missed talking to someone. Sure, I chatted with Nico when I could, but most of our conversations were always rushed. Calculated. I cherish this moment of the getting-to-know-you conversations and savor the feel of our shared touches.

We talk late into the night and fall asleep in each other's arms. We don't bother moving to the bed since our little nest of pillows and moonlight is perfect as is.

Eventually, we both wake up hungry and wander downstairs for another meal, where he properly introduces me to his team.

"Tell me more about your life," I say from the kitchen a few days later as I cook some breakfast for us. We've danced around some of the heavier topics, like how he got the reputation of being the Vampire Slayer, or what I fully endured while in either Dante's or Helios's household. But I swear, something about talking with Zero heals my soul, one tiny piece at a time. It probably has to do with the magical bond that is literally weaving between us. But the more I talk to him, the more I want to know everything I can about my dragon.

"What did you do for the Elite Guard?"

He narrows his eyes.

I laugh, already knowing what he's thinking. "Pretend

I'm not a vampire for a moment. I see the way you talk to your teammates. Tell me about the good things you've done."

"How can you think I've done so much good when I've literally slaughtered your kind?" The worry in his tone is evident. Even though we haven't solidified the bond, or have had sex yet, the magic between us pulses easily. If I had to guess, we were fated before I was taken and the magic started weaving us together back then. It would explain why we've clung onto the idea of each other for so long.

My fingers wrap around the necklace I keep hidden under the hem of my shirt. It was a gift, a pendant carved from the hands of the boy I had a crush on. The boy who did everything in his power to find me once I was taken. The boy I knew, who is now the smart, determined, and loyal man standing in front of me today.

"Don't forget, I know you, Rune. You don't find pleasure in hurting the innocent. Anyone you've killed was supported by the guard."

"Your mate speaks the truth, Zero." Silver appears by my side. His long, straight hair tumbles down to his waist. There are several intricate braids woven throughout the Fae's hair.

Gideon walks into the kitchen and rests his hip against the counter. "Listen to Silver and your mate, Bossman. Everything you've done has helped hundreds, if not thousands, of people."

The four of us spend the next several hours chatting about their missions and the things Zero did for his team. Gideon talks about another teammate who has plans to move into this house, as well as the witch who already lives here but is currently away on a mission.

I learn that Zero built this huge house for his chosen family, and take pleasure in the fact he decorated parts of his house in secret just for me—even though he didn't think I'd ever see it.

When Gideon and Silver wander back up to their rooms, Zero and I take a long walk in his gardens. With our fingers laced, we continue talking, both of us eager to get to know the people we are now and see how it matches up with the friend we used to know.

Chapter Nine

ZERO

"Wake up, Zero." Calix giggles as he yanks back the blinds, the sunlight streaming in through the window. "I have an idea."

I groan dramatically and throw an arm over my eyes to shield my face. "What fresh torture is this? You, my mate, are supposed to be a damn vampire. Sleep in."

Calix climbs onto the bed and yanks the sheet off my body. "Never. Not where there is so much beauty out in the world."

I can't fight the smile that spreads across my face. This beautiful, amazing creature in front of me is so happy, despite everything he's been through. Hell, maybe it's *because* of everything he's been through and how he's now free.

My inner dragon growls. *'Okay, okay,'* I say to my dragon. *'Some of it is also probably thanks to our magical bond.'* I still can't believe our mating bond has started taking root even though we haven't been intimate yet. Gods, we haven't even kissed. And I want Calix with a desperate need, but I also want to prove to him I'm not like those vampires who only used him for his pretty body.

I'm here for the entire package: his looks, fierce personality, and caring nature. His sense of excitement and his brilliant imagination.

When I don't move, Calix continues to complain, unconsciously climbing on top of me and bouncing. I instantly get hard. In his excitement, he doesn't seem to notice.

"So, I have an idea," he starts. "It might sound ridiculous, but I can't stop thinking about it."

I tickle his sides and grin. "Tell me, little mate."

"Do you still like to take photos like you did when we were little? Almost every time I thought about you, I'd imagine you with your camera in hand, and that sweet smile on your face."

"Sweet?" I bark out a laugh. "You think my smile is sweet? I've heard about how charming and sexy I am, but never sweet." I'm happy Calix knows all about the people I slept with over the years. At first, I was hesitant to let him know, but I was determined to tell him before he learned through other means. Calix accepted it easily, laughing and saying he always knew others wouldn't be able to resist my charms.

He then proceeded to tell me he didn't share. If the possessive way he growled that line didn't get me hard, I honestly don't know what else could. The things I want to do to my little mate… I chuckle. And he thinks I'm sweet.

"They're idiots. You are most definitely sweet. Charming? Yes. Flirty? Always. But you've always been such a sweet and caring soul," he says, determination in his tone.

I blink and my lips part with shock. Heat creeps onto my cheeks. No one has ever defended me the way he has. I remember the way he chatted with my teammates as they told stories of our missions. Even when they jokingly said things, not understanding my motives, Calix easily defended me, somehow knowing why I did the things I did while out in the field.

Calix climbs off me and rushes over to my closet. "You never answered the question. Do you still like to take photos?" He holds out a cable-knit sweater and scrunches his left eye as if imagining me in it.

"Yes. It's one of the few things that calms me down," I admit. "Sometimes, I would even pretend you were there with me."

Calix's grin is wide, ocean-blue eyes sparkling.

"Good. Do you remember when we were little, and we used to pretend we were spies?"

I chuckle. "Yes. Of course. I think I remember everything we used to do. We'd walk around town, and I would photograph every single little thing. Some of those photos were absolutely horrible." I laugh. "So many random photos of leaves and rocks."

Calix chuckles as he stands by the bed. He's bouncing on his toes, excited.

"And every time you went with me, you would carry that worn-out little leather journal, and jot down notes about the townsfolk, weaving stories of all the murder and mayhem they were supposedly up to."

Calix bursts into laughter. "Gods, that notebook. It was so ratty. I don't even think it was real leather."

His smile is infectious; something about Calix, in general, is healing to my soul.

"How do you feel about us doing something similar? Bundling up against the cold weather and going out on the town and playing spies?"

"You wanna pretend we're spies?" Fuck, why does the idea of being playful with Calix like this sound so appealing?

"Well, you hardly have to pretend with you being some fancy rogue hunter and all now. But I don't know." He shrugs. "I thought we could go to the town square and get some lunch. Maybe you can bring your camera, and I can bring my notebook. We can spend the day having fun, and people-seeing while we continue getting to know each other again. Maybe we can call it our first official date?"

My heart fucking melts. The idea is so thoughtful and sweet. It's so... us. "I'd like that. A lot."

Calix pauses next to me and pulls out a tiny brown notebook, seemingly out of nowhere. The thing is new and I get the feeling he bought it just for this little impromptu date. He winks, then peers straight ahead. I follow his gaze and chuckle. Almost hidden in a nook between the shops are Blaze, Autumn's brother, and his little demon mate, Cass.

They look lovingly into each other's eyes, and I can't help myself. I pull out my camera and take a photo of the tender look they share. Maybe I can print this and give it to them as a surprise anniversary gift.

Calix is still jotting notes in his notebook, and I get the feeling he might be writing down a plot bunny. I inhale the fresh ocean air of Heart's Hollow. The charming town is a hidden treasure nestled by the Pacific Ocean and surrounded by forest. The magical wards that keep this town hidden will hopefully be expanded soon.

A sense of excitement overcomes me, and I make a mental note to visit Autumn. I hope he can convince the coven to work on the wards sooner rather than later. The thought draws me up short. It's only been a few days since Calix has been returned to me, and the selfish side of me doesn't want him to leave. Would it be weird to ask your fated mate to move in with you so soon after reuniting? Surely, being freaking soulmates doesn't mean we have to apply human norms to our relationship. Right?

Ideas, thoughts, and daydreams swirl around me as we walk downtown. Snow drifts down lazily around us. It's cold out, but the ground is still warm enough that the snow melts as soon as it hits it. Since I'm an amethyst dragon with a literal fire inside of me, and Calix is a vampire, the cold doesn't affect us. Even so, we dress the part. Calix looks so sexy in his peacoat, boots, and thick scarf.

A few two-seater tables are set up outside of our local coffee shop. One of the tables is occupied by a group of witches and a few shifters—all college-age, if I had to guess. One of the shifters makes fur ripple across his arm, and his claws elongate before he shifts back, once again looking fully human. The group cheers, congratulating him on his strength and ability to control a partial shift.

Every time I see something similar in a safe haven town, my heart warms. It's wonderful to witness all these paranormals coexisting peacefully.

"Should we get a coffee to warm up?" Calix asks, waving at the coffee shop's front door.

"You probably aren't even that cold." I laugh. "You just want a coffee, don't you?

Calix's blue eyes sparkle. "Guilty. Come on. My treat."

I still can't believe Nico and Calix had a whole secret bank account hidden from their captor. And to think Calix was making money from the stories he wrote? So cool.

Once we have our drinks, we settle at a table under the awning.

"What are you thinking about?" Calix asks.

"Rook and Autumn are going to freak out when they find out about your pen name."

Calix sits up. "They read my books?" There's the cutest little uplift to his voice, like he's shocked, but also pleasantly surprised. I nod, and his whole face lights up. Then, suddenly, he pulls his notebook out of his pocket and starts jotting down some more notes.

I love that his creative flow seems to be flourishing around me. An image of Calix's notebooks and papers scattered around his writing nook in my bedroom comes to mind. I can totally picture him typing away on a laptop in the little nest of pillows I made for him. My dragon rumbles his approval. Apparently, the domestic daydream is something we both want.

"Move in with me," I blurt. As soon as the words are out, I mentally facepalm. Gods. I don't want to take back the words, but I also don't want to scare him away.

Calix smiles behind the rim of his paper coffee cup and he casually takes a sip.

Brat.

"I talked to Autumn this morning before you woke up. I asked about seeing if we could still try to expand the magical borders, so it reaches my place."

My heart sinks. I always knew that was his plan, but I'd hoped...

"But I asked if he would be willing to let someone new have it. I know there are other vampires out there like me. Humans or witches turned against their will. I want to help them, if it's possible."

"Wait, you talked to Autumn this morning?" I can't fight my grin. "Does this mean you want to move into my place?"

"Of course, I want to move in with you, silly dragon. We're mates. This might be new, and we are still learning everything about each other, but we are also still the same people deep down. I'm still the Calix you met on the playground, and you're still my Rune. Even if dragons and vampires are supposed to be natural enemies."

My heart soars and I scoot my chair closer to his. "Look at us. A real-life *Romeo and Juliet*. But if we're supposed to be enemies, why do I want to kiss you so bad?"

Chapter Ten

CALIX

I suck in a shocked gasp. "You want to kiss me?" I ask, hating the quiver I hear in my voice. Of course, he wants to kiss me. We *are* mates, after all. But I recognized what he was doing as soon as he started giving me room to go on my own terms.

Zero doesn't want to push me, especially knowing what I've been through. But after several days of everything being so close to perfect, a part of me is nervous about rocking the boat. No matter how tempted I am.

I did more research into why vampires and dragons are considered enemies. And the rumors are true; vampires find dragon's blood irresistible. What if we kissed and I couldn't stop myself from trying to bite him?

"You've never been kissed before?"

My mouth falls open, and I narrow my eyes. "Of course, I've been kissed before, it's just—" I snap my mouth shut.

Fuck, what the hell do I even say to that? *I've never kissed anyone I actually wanted to kiss. The only person I've ever wanted to kiss was him?*

"Can we talk about this at home?" I ask. I hate that I just killed the moment, but I need to make sure Zero is safe with me, and I think he can sense my worries through our bond.

Despite me just rejecting our first kiss, Zero melts at my words, and then he smirks. "Yes, little mate. Let's go home."

Thank the gods Heart's Hollow is such a small town. It only takes us about ten minutes to get home. He marches me straight upstairs and into our bedroom.

Gods. Our bedroom. I have never been more excited to share a room with anyone before.

Zero passes the bed and guides me to the arched chaise lounge in the corner of the room. "I want to try something with you," he says as he sits down. He presses his body back so his iridescent wings are against the back cushion. He spreads his legs wide and indicates that he wants me to sit between his legs.

I sit. Then I slowly scoot my body so my back is against his front.

"Close your eyes. Tell me you can feel our magical bond

forming between us."

I nod eagerly, still surprised that our bond started forming without us having sex or going through any mating rituals. "I feel it."

He traces his claws lightly over the inside of my wrist before capturing it in his grasp. With his other hand, he trails a path down my throat. I gasp. The contrast between his sharp claws and light touch causes me to squirm against him.

"You can tell me to stop at any moment," he whispers before sucking on the lobe.

I gasp and nod, squirming more. He's getting hard under me, and it's a heady feeling.

"Keep your eyes closed, Calix. Do you see our magic?" His hand slides under the hem of my sweater. He lazily draws teasing circles on my stomach.

I moan. "I see it. It's—it's beautiful," I pant. "Shades of amethyst blending together with dark blue."

He nods. "Good, vampire. That's us. That's our bond. You can't hurt me. Fate won't let you." He pulls my lobe back between his lips again. I'm fully hard now, grinding against his length. The fingers of his free hand glide over my erection before he pulls away. He lets go of my wrist. I groan in complaint.

"You can do anything you want to me, Calix. I just have one request. Please, kiss me. Please," he begs.

The sudden switch in our power dynamic causes my mind to spin. Zero told me he's always been the one in charge. He knows I was always forced to submit. Even with our first kiss, he's giving me a gift. He's letting me take control.

I flip around and kneel on the chaise, then I climb onto his body, straddling him. He feels so damn good like this. We're still clothed, but somehow, it makes this moment even more erotic. The way my pebbled nipples glide against the soft cloth of my sweater. The feel of his hard erection pressing against his pants, jerking and eager to escape.

Our lips press together as I slant my mouth over his. It's a slow, gentle sweep. Electric heat zaps through my spine, causing me to arch and grind against him. My body demands more. I cup his face in my hands and deepen the kiss.

"So good. You taste better than I imagined." He moans against my lips as his hands reach for my face. A surge of want fills me. With vampiric quickness, I clasp both his wrists in my hands and trap them above his head, pressing them against the chaise. He moans again and I slide my tongue into his mouth. His tongue battles with mine, and I suck it into my mouth. We kiss like we're fighting. It's pure passion.

He's throbbing now, and I like the idea of him coming undone.

Temptation.

Desire.

Lust.

I need to know what he looks like when he comes.

He feels like fire and magic and everything I've ever craved. I grind faster. My body is quivering, desperate to feel him in every way possible. My fangs elongate, and I'm afraid I might lose control. No. Even worse... I want to lose control.

Is this what it feels like to make someone powerful submit to my every whim? For the first time in my life, I am a predator. Zero is my prey, so desperate and needy as he tries to fuck me through our clothes. The feeling is intoxicating. Overwhelming. So fucking addicting.

I let go of his wrists and tug his sweater over his head before yanking my own sweater off. I lick a long path from his collarbone, up his throat, and to his ear. I nip at the tender flesh the way he did to me. He moans.

"You feel like you're ready to come, pretty dragon.

You're so fucking hard for me. Is that true?" I grind against his erection. "Can you come just from this?"

He nods frantically. "Fuck," he whispers. "Yes, Calix."

A sly smirk covers my lips. "Good."

The need to bite him is overwhelming. Helios once told me that sex, blood, and biting go hand in hand. That most of the time we can't have sex without biting. I never felt that need before. But as I sit here grinding on my mate's cock, every muscle inside of me trembles.

Would he let me bite him?

Dragon's blood is supposed to be intoxicating. Can I really stop myself?

As if hearing my thoughts, Zero speaks up. "Bite me. Please, Calix. Please. Like I said, the fact we are fated means your body will know when to stop."

Nothing has ever turned me on as much as my mate begging for my bite. Without another thought, I clasp his jaw with my fingers and tilt his head away. He moans, turning his head easily and giving me his throat. Submitting to me.

I drag my tongue over his neck and feel this huge shifter shiver under my touch. Then I sink my teeth into his throat. He jolts against me, my prey realizing he has fallen into my trap. This dragon is now mine. My heartbeat is pounding. No, wait. Zero's heartbeat is pounding.

I release pleasure down through the bite, only I didn't take into consideration our bond and the intensity of our shared pleasure. I suck at Zero's neck, and he moans so loud I almost come from the pornographic noise he makes. His head is thrown back in ecstasy, and I feel his pleasure as if it's my own as his blood flows into me.

He tastes unlike anything I've ever tasted before. His blood doesn't have that tang of metal I've grown used to. This is sweet and nourishing, like ambrosia. I'm shocked when it only takes a few pulls of his blood to satisfy me completely. Drinking from my dragon reminds me of a rich chocolate mousse, decadent and satisfying, yet I only need a little bit to feel quenched and happy.

I lick his wound closed and continue to grind on him. Zero gasps and moans, completely lost in pleasure as I ride his hard cock as if there isn't any material between us. Before he can register what I'm doing, I decide to surprise my mate by dropping to my knees and tugging his pants off.

His eager cock springs out of his pants, hard and ready. I glance up and lock gazes with his pretty amethyst eyes. He shouts when I wrap my lips around his length. He tastes just as good here as he does everywhere else. I realize that

I'm still pushing pleasure into our shared bond when I reach up and tweak his nipples.

Zero spills into my mouth. I sink down lower as he comes and continues to release down my throat. His orgasm is so intense that I end up coming in my pants thanks to the shared pleasure. Fuck. If things feel this good now, I can only imagine what it would feel like to do this once we were completely mated.

Chapter Eleven

Zero

I wake up to a pleasant warmth wrapped around me, spooning my back. Calix is lightly tracing designs on my chest. Smiling, I hug his slim arms to my chest and my dragon purrs. Is this what happiness feels like? Gods, it's as if I entered an alternate world. Where my sole focus used to be seeking revenge on any rogue vampire I could find, now, my new focus will be taking care of my mate. I'll do this by pleasuring him and providing a safe place for him to live—always.

"Flip over, pretty dragon," he says as he presses a few kisses on my wings. "I want to see your eyes."

I do as I'm told, shocked at how eager I am for my tiny mate's dominance and approval. Then I gasp. My eyes fly to the pendant hanging around his neck. "You kept it?" I ask in a watery tone.

My fingers pick up the dragon pendant I made Calix for

his sixteenth birthday. As I study the intricate design, I'm floored to realize that this dragon is very similar to mine. Did I subconsciously give Calix a piece of my dragon—of me—without knowing?

Joy pulses through our small magical bond. Through all the research I've conducted on my dragon lineage, there is one tradition I crave more than anything: the bonding ceremony. Would Calix entertain the idea? Fate has already deemed us soulmates, but to actually go through a dragon's bonding ceremony would truly mean sharing our souls.

Calix smiles at me. He reaches for the necklace I'm holding, but instead of taking it from me, he wraps his fingers around mine. Together, we hold on to the pendant as Calix's eyes search mine, as if peering inside, learning my deepest thoughts. "I never took it off," he whispers. "You have been with me the entire time."

He's so hauntingly beautiful with his high cheekbones, plush lips, and ocean-blue eyes.

"I still can't believe you're here, Calix. I searched everywhere for you. I never stopped." Tears flood my eyes.

"I know you did, Zero. My beautiful, loyal dragon."

A desperate need to tell him I love him overcomes me, but I push it down. Instead, I try to pour my emotions into a kiss. I pull him to me and devour his lips. This kiss is unlike the first one we shared. This one is just as passionate, but it's tinged with regret. It's filled with apologies. It's filled with all the emotions we are feeding to each other through the bond, but are incapable of voicing at the moment. They're too big, too powerful.

Someday, I hope we'll be able to fully talk about our less-than-pleasant experiences while we were apart. But if not, if we can't, that's okay too. As long as I can wake up every morning with Calix safe and in my bed.

"Zero, I—"

My phone rings, interrupting this serious moment. At first, I ignore it and am about to ask him to continue telling me what he's about to say when it goes off again. I notice it's Gideon, and he would know not to interrupt me so early unless it's important. And considering he isn't knocking on my door, that means he isn't home and must be doing something for the guard.

I hold up my finger to Calix. He smiles and lightly nips at it as I answer my phone. "Hey, Gid. What's going on?"

"I'm so sorry, boss. We need you at the Sinclair Estate. We might have a situation with a rogue."

I sigh. "You know I'm retired, right?"

"Sorry, Zero. It's important. Autumn wanted to talk to

you specifically."

"All right. I'll be there in ten minutes." I hang up the phone, sighing.

"Is everything okay?" Calix asks.

I nod. "Yeah, Elite Guard business. Will you be okay if I take care of this?"

"Yes, go be a hero," he says, pressing a kiss against my lips. "I have a few things I need to finish up, anyway."

I chuckle. "No more hero stuff. I'm retired. That means no more missions. But if this is regarding me building a safe house, I'll be glad to work in our town, knowing I get to come home to you every day."

"Gods, you're so cheesy," Calix teases.

"Hey! Hush you. It's your fault." I tickle his sides until he begs for mercy. "Text me if you leave the house. I'll be back as soon as I can."

The further I drive away from my house, the more I feel our magical bond strain, causing my dragon to whine. I didn't realize that an incomplete bond could do this. I guess it must be a dragon thing. My inner dragon huffs.

Mate. Bond. Bite. "Okay, buddy," I say out loud as I rub my chest. "We'll at least talk to Calix about the mating process when we get home." There was no way in hell I would go through with the mating bite or a bonding ceremony without his full consent. Not after the way Helios treated him.

I pull into Sinclair Estate and chuckle. Autumn had the audacity to say my place was big. Yet, his family's estate has me beaten—*by a long shot*. As soon as I park and jog up to the front door, I knock. Someone guides me inside and shows me to a room where I find Autumn, Gideon, and several coven members I vaguely recognize.

Autumn rushes forward with a smile and hugs me. "Hey, thanks for coming. We have a bit of a situation."

One of the coven members walks forward with another witch by his side. Autumn makes quick introductions. "Zero, this is Nico. He's—"

"Calix's friend," I gasp. "It's so nice to meet you. Thank you for making that potion for my mate."

Nico instantly relaxes. "Gods, Autumn told me that Calix met his mate, but when I found out who it was, I was scared it was a trick. But if he told you I made the potion, then I know he trusts you."

My dragon sits up with pride. "Thank you. That means

a lot to me. So, how can I help everyone today?"

Autumn points at a chair and I take a seat. "The main reason we wanted you here is because of your skill. There's been a vampire who has been trying to break through Heart's Hollow's wards."

My eyes widen.

"Don't worry, he hasn't been able to breach the wards, but he's persistent, and it's draining some of our power. We can hold it up, but we want him gone. If he's this desperate, he might be willing to hurt anyone who walks past the magical protection."

"Okay, that makes sense. But Gideon and my team have dealt with similar missions. Why did you need me?"

Nico speaks up. "There's something else we need to tell you."

My heart skips a beat. What the fuck is going on?

"The rogue trying to break through the wards is Dante. Calix's maker."

I stand abruptly, my chair toppling over. That's when I feel it. Panic and fear pulsing through the bond. Yanking my phone out of my pocket, the blood drains from my face when I see a text from Calix.

> Calix: I'm going to my place in the woods. I want to grab some clothes and see if anything is salvageable in the wreckage. I'll be back in fifteen.

Suddenly, a blinding pain hits the back of my head. No. Not my head. Calix. The bond flickers between us, then winks out.

There's nothing.

Nothing.

Darkness.

I can't feel the bond. At all.

My dragon roars with outrage.

Chapter Twelve

CALIX

A LARGE, SHARP ROCK is jabbing me in the side. I swallow roughly. Where the hell am I? Stemming my panic, I try to think. Memories slowly start trickling in. The last thing I remember was waking up in bed holding my mate. Despite the pain in my side and the throbbing in my head, I want to smile. Only I can't, because the throbbing pain in the back of my head is excruciating.

I remember walking through the forest, admiring the white glitter of the snowflakes as they floated to the ground. The door to my house was open again, but this time, there was a light on. Someone was inside. I slowly backed away and pulled out my phone. I was about to call Zero for help when I saw him.

Dante.

My heart pounds at the memory. His command not

to move. The way I was unable to disobey my sire's compulsion. The fury raged through me as he walked behind me and knocked me out with something.

"Finally, you're awake," Dante snarls, the whites of his eyes bulging.

I blink. There's something wrong with him. He seems manic... crazed.

"Dante," I say slowly. "What am I doing here?"

He screeches. The noise pierces a sharp pain through my ears. I attempt to grab my head, but realize I'm tied up. Stealthily, I the ropes and sigh in relief when I find that in Dante's haste—or carelessness—he did a haphazard job of restraining me. Not to mention, if I work some of it loose, my vampire strength should be able to break through them.

I take a deep breath and try to clear my mind. Focusing on trying to push the pain away, I take in my surroundings. Another moment of relief. We aren't far from my house, maybe a few miles away. I remember this tiny cave from my hunts through the forest.

Dante mumbles to himself. His movements are disjointed and strange.

"Dante," I repeat. "What am I doing here? What's going on?" Did he figure out I killed Helios and he's captured me to seek revenge?

"I'm here to collect you, my little doll."

I flinch when I hear his nickname for me, then I see red. Snarling against my bonds, I infuse the red-hot fury into my words. "Don't ever fucking call me that again." Using all the rage I can manage, I struggle against the ropes, but in the process, I feel one of the knots tighten. *Fuck.* I probably made it worse.

I let out another slow breath.

Dante laughs. "Little doll, little doll. I'm here to play," he singsongs. "I am ready to play with my little doll. The one with the beautiful golden hair."

He plops down next to me and starts tapping his fingers onto his thighs. He hums along a rhythm to a silent song only he can hear. I freeze. He's completely unhinged. I let myself study Dante for a moment, seeing tattoos and scratches all over his arms.

My eyes widen in understanding. He's been trying to break through the wards. The magic must be able to detect what he wants to do to me. I shudder. It must be really bad if the wards are affecting him from outside the town's limits.

As I continue working on trying to untie the ropes, Dante keeps humming to himself eerily. When I don't have much success, I close my eyes and concentrate on the magical bond between Zero and me. A hollow gnawing pain rolls through my stomach and I still.

I'm ravenous.

My mouth falls open and I can feel my fangs completely extended outward. I'm unable to retract my fangs.

Fuck. I'm literally starving to death.

Dante continues to hum as he rocks back and forth, scratching at his tattoos.

How long have I been in this cave?

Chapter Thirteen
ZERO

It's been days. Literal fucking days. Dante must be one smart vampire mother fucker because he paid some dirty witch a shit ton of money to perform several spells for him, preventing him from being tracked.

Then he killed her before she could even take advantage of her big payout.

Dante is obsessed with my mate.

We have my whole team on this mission to find Calix, but we don't have a single clue. The asshole owns several properties, and my teammates have raided all of them. The only reason I haven't been able to raid the houses with them is because my dragon goes on a rampage anytime we get a certain distance away from Heart's Hollow.

I punch a hole in a wall inside my house. Luckily, I can tell that Calix is alive, but barely. For some reason my mate keeps going in and out of consciousness, so there's no real way for me to communicate with him.

I have only ever been this terrified once before in my life—fifteen years ago, the first time Calix was taken by this mother fucker. My only flicker of hope is the fact that my dragon doesn't want to leave the general area, which gives me the feeling that my mate is still relatively close. The only problem is where? With literal spells preventing us from tracking Dante and Calix, we don't know where to look, not to mention it feels like we've already looked everywhere, anyway.

"Where the fuck is my mate?" I snarl at the moon.

Taking a deep breath for what feels like the millionth time, I concentrate on my inner dragon and what he senses. That's when I feel some type of... magical tug. Excitement rushes through me. My dragon is guiding me forward. For the last several weeks, my dragon and I have worked hard to communicate better. I've worked tirelessly to have more trust in my dragon.

I immediately text my team, telling them to track me through my phone. Then I follow the tug like an enchanted trail of breadcrumbs. When I leave my property and start walking down the street, the pull gets stronger, causing me to break out into a jog as I leave my neighborhood. I weave my way through the 'downtown' of Heart's Hollow, hopeful that I'm onto something.

I pause in front of a random shop. Everything in me can sense a strange power encouraging me to walk through the door. I glance up and realize that I'm back in front of The Magic Shop. I try the handle, and I'm shocked to find the door unlocked.

Walking into the dimly lit shop, that sense of rightness hits me. The familiar, comforting scent of incense and books fills my lungs, but disappointment washes over me at the same time—Calix isn't here.

"Welcome back, young dragon." The Owner descends a staircase and walks up to me. He's dressed to the nines in his fitted black suit, top hat, and all.

I open my mouth to correct him, but he holds up a slender hand. "Zero, yes. I remember. I'm glad you've made it back to my shop. It looks like you've learned to trust your inner dragon, after all."

Inside my chest, my dragon puffs with pride. I nod, giving The Owner a small smile before glancing around again.

A sense of defeat hits me. If Calix isn't here, why am I? I can feel the bond straining, indicating that I'm now further away from him. If I can feel this, then why the hell can't I pinpoint his location? Is it the spell Dante is using? Or maybe the fact that we aren't fully bonded?

Frustrated, angry tears fill my eyes. Why the hell didn't I tell him I loved him? I just got him back, and now he might be taken from me again. Trembling with rage, I collapse into a heap on the floor next to The Owner. All this rage, and nowhere to put it. All this fear and emotion rampaging through me, and I don't know what to do with it.

My amethyst scales ripple across my arms and I fight my dragon, willing him not to shift.

"I sensed you coming, Zero," The Owner says, kneeling close to me. Our eyes meet and his black eyes search my face.

"I need your help," I croak. "My mate. A rogue took my mate. *Again*."

When realization suddenly dawns on me, a few tears escape. "I'm that seventeen-year-old kid again, and the same rogue vampire has destroyed my world, has taken the one person who is my everything away from me. Fifteen years later, and I'm still completely helpless."

My dragon tries to shift again. I fight it, not wanting to destroy this mystical shop.

The Owner continues to study me silently before he

finally speaks. "Do you remember what I told you about the judgment card?"

I nod, closing my eyes. I practically memorized his words, taking all the lessons to heart. This new chapter of my life was also a new chapter for Calix, and just like that, it's been ripped away from us.

"Why did you run out of the store that first day we met? The day you reunited with your mate?"

I purse my lips, not even shocked he somehow seems to know everything. "I think I ran because I realized I was the one who pulled the card in reverse."

The Owner nods. "And what did I say about your card? What message did you absorb?"

"Self-doubt. I'm my biggest critic, and I must be the one ignoring my true calling." I ponder the words, and everything suddenly falls into place, almost like tiny puzzle pieces finding their match. I already know what to do. *Holy shit. I know what to do.* I need to shift. My dragon hums excitedly in my chest.

"Well, what are you waiting for? Stop ignoring it," he says simply, eyes sparkling. "I can tell you already figured it out."

I *blink*.

The Owner points at the scales rippling across my arms.

"Stop fighting your shift and doubting yourself."

My mouth falls open as he confirms what I was already thinking. I throw my arms around The Owner and kiss his temple. His top hat tips to the side, but he catches it with a laugh. "Now, go find your mate, young dragon."

Chapter Fourteen

Zero

I rush toward the front door and storm outside, accidentally slamming into Gideon.

He hits the ground. *Hard.* "Fuck, Bossman, what's going on?"

Silver appears by Gideon's side and extends his hand as he helps the demigod stand up—not that a little asphalt could take out someone as powerful as Gideon.

"I can't believe I didn't think of this before. We need to get to a clearing," I shout. "I have to shift."

Silver arches a brow, but they follow me as I take off down the alley and toward the back parking lot. Luckily, my dragon is only the size of a large van. As I run, I yank off my jacket and shirt, then hand my wallet and phone to Gideon.

"Why are you shifting?" Silver asks.

"I need to stop doubting myself," I murmur, before

speaking up. "Dragons aren't usually affected by a witch's magic. If I shift, I can fly overhead, and I might be able to sense Calix." I skid to a stop and tug off my pants. I toss them to Silver.

"Take Gideon with you. You need one of us for backup. Gid can carry your phone, and I can track your location."

I nod, thankful my friends are here. "All right. You ready?"

Gideon nods eagerly. "Hell yeah! I love flying."

Silver shudders next to us. The Fae have always hated being airborne.

My dragon throws himself against my ribcage, and scales ripple along my arms. He's eager to get out. Eager to take to the wind and find our mate. Without a second thought, I let the shift take over. Scales erupt all over my body, my wings expand, and I fall to all fours. The shift is always painful, but it's over within seconds.

Gideon places my phone in his jacket pocket, zips it closed, and wraps his arms around my neck. Climbing effortlessly onto my back is something we have down pat. I crouch low to the ground, then spring into the air, taking flight.

Gideon whoops with joy as I aim for the sky.

It takes longer than I hoped, but finally I feel my bond

with Calix. Worry pulses through me at the faint magic. Something is very wrong with my mate.

I think he's dying.

I bite back a sob, knowing he needs me at my best.

We soar through the air until I'm hovering over a spot in the forest. From this angle, I can see a small cave opening. Gideon must spot it too, because his grip on me tightens. Once he has a decent grip, I dive toward the ground. Since I'm a dragon, there's no real way for me to land quietly, especially with someone on my back.

I land with a thump and shift back. Gideon tosses my clothes at me and in record time, I have my pants and sweater on. I don't bother zipping it closed. We fall into formation and take to the shadows. Sneaking up on a vampire is nearly impossible, but we move quietly and efficiently, just in case Dante is distracted.

When I enter the cave, I spot the rogue easily, but I draw up short when I notice him rocking manically on the ground. Knees curled up to his chest. Gideon's eyes whip toward mine, and I silently communicate that I have no idea what's going on. We move forward, and I listen with all my senses. I'm pretty sure Dante is the only rogue.

Movement catches my eye. It's Calix. He blinks his large blue eyes my way and whimpers weakly.

"Calix!" I cry out, rushing to his side. I throw myself onto the ground next to him and immediately start working on the knots at his wrists. Thank the gods, it's only rope. But why hasn't he snapped through them himself?

Not wanting to hurt him, just in case, I work quickly but efficiently to untie his bindings. Briefly, I glance up at Gideon and nod toward the crazed rogue still rocking on the ground. "Kill him," I snarl. "I don't want my mate to see his face ever again."

Gideon nods. Without hesitation, he uses his demigod strength and rips the rogue's head from his body, then tosses it to the ground just as Dante disintegrates to ash.

As soon as the knots are loose, Calix crumples to the ground. "Oh, gods. Baby, talk to me. What's wrong?"

"Sta—starving," he rasps.

Fuck. There is a sunken slump to his body, dark bags under his eyes, his fangs are extended, and his lips are chapped. My mate is starving to death. My dragon roars in my chest, banging violently against my ribcage. Anger fuels us both, but I use that rage to slash my wrist with my claws. Then, I let my vampire feed from me.

He's too weak to pour pleasure into me, thank goodness. I *need* to feel the pain. I *need* to know I'm helping my mate. Eventually, Calix begins sucking at my wrist. He starts off with tiny, weak suckles, drinking slowly until they finally turn into healthy pulls.

I'm vaguely aware of Silver arriving with backup. Silver mentions something about blood bags, but I shoo him away.

I press tiny kisses into Calix's hair and murmur sweet nothings, hoping he can hear what I'm saying. Once I feel pleasure pouring through our bond, I know everything will be okay. Calix will be okay.

Smiling, I close my eyes and let my vampire drink his fill.

Chapter Fifteen

CALIX

Is this what heaven feels like? The scent of cinnamon and cloves fills my lungs. I inhale deeply while I continue to feed. Light kisses touch my hair, and the sweetest praise is whispered into my ear.

I blink my eyes open and see my mate. My dragon.

For the first time in days, I feel strong.

I pull my fangs out of my mate's wrist and lick the wound closed.

"See," he grins at me. "I told you that you couldn't hurt me."

For the first time in weeks, I feel brave.

Tracing my fingers over Zero's amethyst wings, I remember the way he soared over the forest. His dragon was so beautiful from the cave's opening. *I knew he would come.*

"I love you, Zero."

He helps me stand before tipping my mouth up to his. Zero pours all his emotions through our shared bond. I smile against his lips.

For the first time in years, I feel loved.

I'm beaming up at Zero as he gathers me into his arms. Despite my newfound strength, I curl into his side and close my eyes. "Will you take me home now?"

For the first time ever, I feel safe.

"I love you, too, Calix." He presses another kiss against my lips. "My beautiful, beautiful vampire." Zero gazes into my eyes.

Like a fire blazing through our souls, absolution shines within our bond.

"Let's go home."

EPILOGUE

CALIX

MOONLIGHT STREAMS THROUGH OUR bedroom window a few nights later. Nerves and excitement flicker through my body. Tonight, Zero and I are completing our mating bond. After returning home from the cave, Zero and I spent the night cuddled up together in our little nest, chatting, feeding each other grapes, and making out like teenagers.

While I'm grateful for my vampire healing, I'm pretty sure Zero's blood is the real reason I feel so good. Or hell, it could have been because of our bond, or maybe the joy bouncing between us at being reunited. Either way, it's all because of Zero in my book.

That night, Zero and I confessed our love to each

other over and over again. We both needed to hear it several times after being separated for so long and not knowing if I would survive. Zero told me more about his dragon traditions. He explained the bonding ritual of making love, the bite, and how a fated mate can accept a dragon's scale into their body, forever entwining their souls together.

He told me he wanted me to consider it someday and explained how much he craved that type of bond. I'm so proud of him for speaking the truth. Because I don't need to think about it. I want that. I want him. *Forever*.

Call us cheesy romantics, but that night, we decided the first time we made love would be the night we bonded. I wanted to do it immediately, but Zero wanted to give me a few days to think about it. I fell even deeper in love with him because of it, too. He's always making me feel so cherished and appreciated, never wanting me to feel pressured because of our bond.

Zero steps into the bedroom and slowly undoes the buttons on his black button-down shirt. He exposes his chest first, adorned with all those pretty amethyst scales. His pierced nipples are next, followed by his toned abs. My dragon is a sexy piece of art and a snack all rolled into one.

He smirks. "Do you like what you see, little vampire?"

I grin. "You know I do. Now, stop making me wait." I pat the bed next to me. "Get over here, dragon."

He continues to strip, giving me a show. My cock jerks with excitement. Gods, the way he can make my whole body react is just so unfair. Zero peels his tight pants off his thick thighs and his hard cock springs forward. Damn.

Two can play that game. I slide the silky sheet off my body, exposing my naked flesh to him, bit by bit.

His pupils dilate, then flicker into slits. Zero growls when I'm fully exposed and strides forward with dragon speed, kneeling on the floor in front of me. Who knew such a large, confident dragon would like to submit?

"Tell me what to do, love," Zero whispers, his cock hard and eager in front of him. Fuck. A vampire can get used to such a sight.

I lay back on the bed and prop my foot on his shoulder. "Open me up with your tongue. Get me ready for you."

Zero growls again, before diving forward and doing just that as he buries his face between my thighs. He takes his time lapping, licking, and teasing. He groans and slowly strokes himself as he feasts on me. If I didn't have a specific goal in mind, I would be tempted to see if I could come just from this. I smirk.

Next time.

Only once I'm whimpering, mewing, and absolutely desperate for my mate's cock, do I finally give his head a light push so his mouth is no longer on me. "Enough," I pant. "I want you inside of me."

He groans. "Gods, your scent. I finally figured out what it is." He surges forward and licks a path up my throat.

I shiver. "Isn't that a mate thing? You're supposed to smell like something delicious to your fated?"

Zero nods as he breathes me in. "What do I smell like to you?" His hand trails down to my hard length and slowly strokes me. Teases me. Fuck, he feels so good. I'm throbbing for him.

"Cloves," I gasp. "You smell like cinnamon and cloves. What about me? What do I smell like?"

"Like dragon fruit," he hums, clearly lust drunk.

I burst into laughter. Only my cocky dragon would have a mate that smells like dragon fruit.

He growls and pushes into me.

"Yes!" I cry out when he bottoms out. "Harder."

Fucking finally. My hips thrust forward.

He reaches under me, pulls my body to his, and starts pounding into me. I'm fire and heat, the passion burning inside of me.

More.

More.

More.

Fuck, I need more. I lightly push my hand against his stomach. Making a face, he pulls his cock out of me, and I smirk. "I'm going to ride you now, pretty dragon."

With my vampire speed and strength, I pull my body away from his, flip him over so he's flat on the bed, and then straddle him. Once I'm fully seated on his cock, he groans. Then I start riding him. I move my hips in a tantalizing circle, determined to drive him—and myself—crazy.

He sucks in a deep breath when I lean forward to grasp his wrists, placing them above his head. I trap him there for a few minutes as I continue to work him over. When I let go of his wrists, I use both my hands to start tugging on his nipple rings until the nipples are red and puffy.

Then I simply ride him with inhuman speed, determined to make us both come.

I watch, transfixed by his piercings, his toned abs, and the way his chest rises and falls faster and faster as he gets closer to the edge. His gaze drops to where my *very* erect cock is dripping onto his stomach, and his amethyst eyes turn into dragon slits.

"Stroke me, love."

His claw-tipped hands wrap around me. All it takes is three strokes, and I'm spilling all over him as I shudder apart.

He roars. "Fuck. So tight." Hot liquid heat erupts inside of me.

"I'm ready," I gasp, still coming.

He yanks me down to him and bites his claiming mark into my neck. I instantly orgasm again, and so does he.

Memories flicker through our bond. That first day I saw Rune on the playground. The look on his face when he gifted me my dragon pendant. The moment we picked up the same tarot card in the magic shop. Our first kiss. The joy I felt when I saw his dragon flying above the cave, there to rescue me.

My love for this man is boundless.

He collapses back onto the bed.

A scale falls off his chest, shining brighter than the rest. An offering. I lift his scale to the light, admiring the way it shimmers; like magic and starlight. I place it against my chest, above my heart. Love and magic playfully whirl and spin between us before the scale disappears into my chest as I magically absorb it into my soul.

Purple flames lick across my skin, like sparks of lust

igniting between us. His dragon's flame.

"You're immune now, and our souls are one." He smiles up at me.

Mate. Mate. Mate. I hear his dragon in my head. No, not his dragon. *Our* dragon.

Emotions overwhelm me. "I love you, Zero.

"I love you too, little vampire."

THE END

Thank you for reading Zero and Calix's story. If you're curious about Autumn and Rook, you can find their story in **Love Potions and Moonlight.**

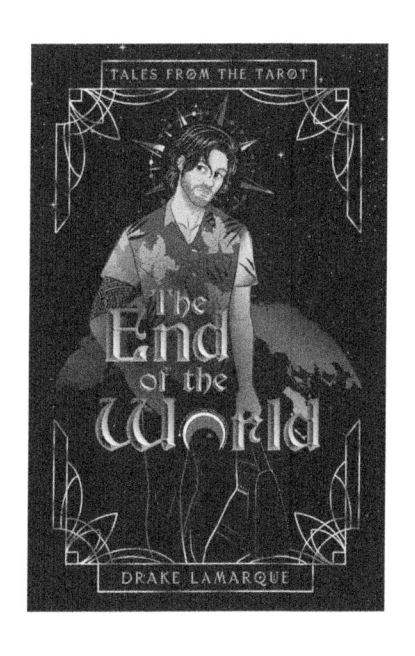

WHAT'S NEXT?

books2read.com/theEndoftheWorld

Ash has traveled the globe. Will he ever find what he's looking for?

Travel influencer Ash has made running from his

problems his career—until his journey comes to an end. Back home in Aotearoa New Zealand, Ash knows he's expected to finally settle down, a thought that fills him with nothing but dread. If this is what he really wants…why does it make him feel so empty?

When Hallow, a fairy-like man, travels out of Ash's dream to quite literally land in his lap, Ash realises he has bigger problems than his inability to settle down.

A powerful monster pursues Hallow, preventing him from returning home. Forget jet-lag. If he is to help Hallow, Ash is going to need a crash course in magic, inter-dimensional travel and—love?

TALES FROM THE TAROT

**Grab the 22-book series at
mybook.to/talesfromthetarot**

Where Fools Have Tread by Jennifer Cody
The Magician's Heart by J.P. Jackson
Cleric of Desire by Amanda Meuwissen
The Nephilim's Touch by Morgan Lysand
King of Hollywood by Fae Quin

My Minotaur Daddy by Laura Lascarso
Across Space & Time by Kit Barrie
Chariot of Souls by Morgan Mason
By Rude Strength by K.L. Hiers
Found in Obscurity by A.M. Rose
Twisted Fates by Adam J. Ridley
No Justice for the Damned by Hellie Heat
The Angel's Kiss by Nicholas Bella
Death Song by B. Ripley
Arcanum by Ashlyn Drewek
The Devil's Dilemma by Alex J. Adams
Camelot's Tower by Brooke Matthews
A Highland Gargoyle's Lucky Star by Chloe Archer
Trust in the Moon by Delaney Rain
Raising the Sun by Eryn Hawk
Zero Judgment by Kota Quinn
The End of the World by Drake LaMarque

About the Author

Kota Quinn writes sweet and steamy MM stories that range from small-town romance to daddy kink, omegaverse, and paranormal romance. Kota can usually be found running errands with a pair of headphones on and a coffee in hand.

Also By
Kota Quinn

Love Potions and Moonlight
Cursed Wolf and Sassy Witch

The Fallen Anthology
*Short story. Limited time.
Will be published by itself in 2025*

The Ringmaster
A low-angst, enemies-to-lovers romance between a half-fae/half-demon and a cursed human

...and more at Amazon.com

Printed in Great Britain
by Amazon